● ● ● ● ● ●

"Bitch, you need to get whatever you came in here for and get the hell on with that bullshit. Ain't nobody finna take off they clothes fo' yo ass."

Her smile didn't falter.

"Oh, you ain't?"

"Hell naw! You want me to pull my pockets out, I *might* do that. But I ain't finna get naked, just 'cause you got a motherfucking gun pointed at me. If you was on some murder shit, you woulda did it by now."

The woman sighed, and her smile slipped this time. "You really testing my patience."

"*I don't give a fuck about yo motherfucking patience.* What's really going on? You wanna see my dick, or something?"

Her eyes flashed slightly.

"Oh, that's it, ain't it?" the short man said. The corner of his mouth curved into a smile. "You heard about a nigga and wanna see if it's true."

She humored him. "See if what's true?"

"See if my dick really that big."

She couldn't stop herself from chuckling. "Yeah, I guess so. Is it really that big? Show me."

Without hesitation, the short man unbuckled his pants and pushed them midway down his thighs, boxers included. That almost wasn't far enough to make it past his piece, which was more *bizarre* than impressive. He easily surpassed the desired length for a porn star, and he wasn't even erect. As tense as the moment was, the woman couldn't snatch her eyes away from the monstrosity between his legs.

The man's smile broadened. "Yeah, I knew that's what you wanted. Why don't you put that gun down, and let me show you what it do. I'll let bygones be bygones, and you can walk up outta here, if you let me fuck the shit outta yo lil' ass. You gon' be walking bowlegged, but at least you'll be alive."

The woman snorted slightly. Her expression did not change as she lowered her weapon. Midway down, all three men were shocked by the loud report.

● ● ● ● ● ●

ASHA AND BOOM PART 3

KEITH THOMAS WALKER

KEITHWALKERBOOKS, INC

KEITHWALKERBOOKS

Publishing Company
KeithWalkerBooks, Inc.
P.O. Box 690
Allen, TX 75013

ISBN-13 DIGIT: 978-1-7356151-1-0
ISBN-10 DIGIT: 1-7356151-1-0
Library of Congress Control Number: 2021912650
Manufactured in the United States of America

Visit us at www.keiththomaswalker.com

KEITH THOMS WALKER

This book is for Janae

CONTENTS

TEASER
TITLE PAGE
COPYRIGHT
DEDICATION
MORE BOOKS BY KEITH THOMAS WALKER
PROLOGUE: B.D.
CHAPTER 1
CHAPTER 2
CHAPTER 3
CHAPTER 4
PART ONE: DOG MAN
CHAPTER 5
CHAPTER 6
CHAPTER 7
CHAPTER 8
CHAPTER 9
CHAPTER 10
CHAPTER 11
CHAPTER 12
PART TWO: AN OLD FACE
CHAPTER 13
CHAPTER 14
CHAPTER 15
CHAPTER 16
CHAPTER 17
CHAPTER 18
CHAPTER 19
CHAPTER 20
CHAPTER 21

PART THREE: LOOSE LIPS
CHAPTER 22
CHAPTER 23
CHAPTER 24
CHAPTER 25
CHAPTER 26
CHAPTER 27
CHAPTER 28
CHAPTER 29
PART FOUR: NONCOMMITTAL
CHAPTER 30
CHAPTER 31
CHAPTER 32
CHAPTER 33
CHAPTER 34
CHAPTER 35
CHAPTER 36
PART FIVE: REAL TEARS
CHAPTER 37
CHAPTER 38
CHAPTER 39
CHAPTER 40
CHAPTER 41
CHAPTER 42
CHAPTER 43
CHAPTER 44
CHAPTER 45
PART SIX: NON-BELIEVER
CHAPTER 46
CHAPTER 47
CHAPTER 48
CHAPTER 49

CHAPTER 50
CHAPTER 51
CHAPTER 52
CHAPTER 53
EPILOGUE
CHAPTER 54
CHAPTER 55
ABOUT THE AUTHOR

MORE BOOKS BY KEITH THOMAS WALKER

Blurred Lines: The Monster
Blurred Lines: Cop Killer
Blurred Lines: Copycat Killer
Blurred Lines: Mister Me Too

Asha and Boom Part 1
Asha and Boom Part 2
Asha and Boom Part 3

Backslide
Backslide 2

The Realest Ever
The Realest Christmas Ever

Prom Night at Finley High
Fast Girls at Finley High
Bullies at Finley High

Jackson Memorial
Jackson Memorial 2

Brick House
Brick House 2
Brick House 3

Threesome
Threesome 2

Take One of Mine
Take one of Mine Part 2

Fixin' Tyrone
How to Kill Your Husband
A Good Dude
Riding the Corporate Ladder
The Finley Sisters' Oath of Romance
Blow by Blow
Jewell and the Dapper Dan
Harlot
Plan C (And More KWB Shorts)
Dripping Chocolate
Sleeping With the Strangler
Life After
Blood for Isaiah
One on One
Election Day
Evan's Heart
Poor Righteous Poet
Might be Bi Part One
Harder
Primal Part One
Hotline Fling

Visit www.keiththomaswalker.com for information about
these and upcoming titles from KeithWalkerBooks

PROLOGUE
B.D.

CHAPTER
1

THE PIT STOP wasn't much of a club. It wasn't much of a pool hall either, though six pool tables were aligned in three rows of two, and pool playing was the primary activity for patrons who visited the locale for more than the few minutes it took to complete a transaction. The Pit Stop was a decent bar, complete with cheap liquor and watered-down variants of top shelf concoctions, which was typical of the dives in this west side neighborhood.

The Pit Stop was closed for business at a quarter till 3am on a Tuesday night, but three men remained inside the dank, dimly lit building. Two of the men were co-owners of the establishment. The third was the closest they had to an official accountant. This man counted and stacked a moderate pile of money on the bar top. The other two men sorted bags of various narcotics on one of the pool tables before placing them in duffle bags.

The Pit Stop was not a dope house, as no dope was ever cooked there, and few transactions took place at this location. But it was certainly more of a dope house than it was a club, pool hall or bar.

Alerted by a knock on the door of the main entrance, the money-counter's eyes narrowed. The men at the pool table hurriedly placed the remaining narcotics in the duffle bags. The shorter man of the two placed the bags on the floor, out of view, and reached for a chrome Glock 40 that rested near the corner pocket. The other man made his way to the door.

Once there, he peered through the peephole and then looked back and told his cohorts, "It's a bitch."

"The fuck she want?" the man with the pistol asked.

"*The fuck you want?*" the man at the door shouted. "We closed."

"Sky sent me," the woman on the other side announced. "Ain't it time for y'all's nightcap?"

"You told Sky to send some bitches over here?" the man with the gun asked.

The one at the door shook his head. "Naw."

"How many of 'em is it?" the one with the gun asked.

The man at the door looked again and said, "It's just one."

"Tell that bitch we straight."

"Hold up, she look good?" the accountant asked as he made his way around the bar.

The one at the door checked the peephole again. "Yeah, she look good. I can't see her whole body, though. *Hey, step back,*" he said through the door. "Let me see what you working with."

Their visitor complied. The man at the door saw that in addition to her fair skin, which was his preference, she was slim with moderate curves.

"Turn around," he said. "Lemme see that ass."

She followed his instructions, and he smiled. He looked back at his running buddies.

"She ain't all that, but she got a nice lil' onion. I wanna hit."

"You *always* wanna hit," the man with the gun said. "I guess you want yo dick sucked too," he said to the accountant, who had made his way to the foyer by then.

"Do a bear shit in the woods?" the accountant replied, his shifty eyes twinkling.

"Why you come by yourself?" the man at the door asked, smiling. "It's a bunch of niggas in here. You finna get us all straight?"

"I can only do three at a time," the woman said, turning back towards the door. "That's all the holes I got."

The doorman's eyes lit up as he studied her features. She was dead serious.

"Lemme see this bitch," the man with the gun said. He was so short, his eyes barely reached the peephole without him standing on his toes. But he saw enough to pique his interest.

Most of Sky's bitches were pretty, but this was the first one he would go as far as calling *beautiful*, which was saying something, because out of all the women he knew, only his daughter was worthy of that description. Thinking of shoving his unsheathed dick between her lips – the ho was in for a rude awakening, if she expected him to get some head with a condom on – he undid the locks and pulled the door open.

He was surprised, but not completely surprised, to see the woman had produced a pistol, seemingly out of nowhere. She breached the doorway before he had a chance to slam it closed or raise his own weapon. Her face was completely different now. Rather than beautiful, her expression was sinister. Her eyes were deathly serious, as was the business end of her weapon. She shoved it against his forehead before he could make out the caliber.

"Y'all niggas back up," she barked at the other two, without taking her eyes off the gunman. "Drop that shit, nigga," she ordered. When he hesitated, her eyes grew even more vicious. She told him, "You know as well as I do that you ain't gon' get no shots off before I blow yo brains out. If you wanna die, just say so, and we can get this shit over with right now. Either way, I'ma leave here with the money. If I gotta step over yo dead body on my way out, it don't make me no never mind. *I told y'all niggas to back up*!" she shouted at the other two.

The man with the gun flinched, thinking she'd ended his life when she shouted. When he realized she hadn't pulled the trigger, rather than relief, his sneer deepened.

"You gon' die," he said assuredly.

"You got one second," she said, glaring at him. "I'm done talking."

He dropped the gun.

"*Now back up*!" she ordered. She reached back with her leg and kicked the door closed when he moved away from her.

With the men lined up a respectable distance away, she was able to assess them individually. The one she'd disarmed was the shorter of the three. He had short hair, dark skin and a stocky frame. The one she assumed she'd initially been speaking to through the door was the tallest. He was lanky and handsome, despite his wide nose and beady eyes. The one standing furthest away was dark and shifty. He gave her the most anxiety, even though he wasn't armed, and the shorter man was more aggressive.

In return, the men had time to take in her features. The woman who had the gall to pull this move wore a weave or a bad wig that hung down to her shoulders. Her tank top had a plunging neckline and ran out of fabric a couple of inches above her belly button. Her cut off shorts were form fitting and shredded, showing off plenty of succulent thigh meat. She was more skinny than fine, but her attractiveness was undeniable. The strap of her purse hung over her neck, crossing her body. The purse didn't look large enough to conceal the weapon she pointed at them, but there was no doubt that's where she had concealed it. She definitely didn't have a gun in her hand when the handsome man asked her to step back and show off her physique.

"You fucking with the wrong one," the short man said. "You might make it outta here with some money, but you ain't gon' live long enough to spend it. The timer on yo life started ticking the moment you came in here."

"Damn," the woman said and grinned. "That shit was almost poetic. You just came up with that line, or you been saving it for a time like this? You don't look smart enough to be so witty."

The man gritted his teeth and fumed. The woman gave him something to really be upset about.

"I need y'all to strip. Butt naked. Take everything off, even yo socks."

The men traded glances with each other, rather than respond or remove any of their clothing. The shorter man, who was clearly the leader, was the first to look her in the eyes and offer a rebuttal.

"Bitch, you need to get whatever you came in here for and get the hell on with that bullshit. Ain't nobody finna take off they clothes fo' yo ass."

Her smile didn't falter.

"Oh, you ain't?"

"Hell naw! You want me to pull my pockets out, I *might* do that. But I ain't finna get naked, just 'cause you got a motherfucking gun pointed at me. If you was on some murder shit, you woulda did it by now."

The woman sighed, and her smile slipped this time. "You really testing my patience."

"*I don't give a fuck about yo motherfucking patience. What's really going on? You wanna see my dick, or something?*"

Her eyes flashed slightly.

"Oh, that's it, ain't it?" the short man said. The corner of his mouth curved into a smile. "You heard about a nigga and wanna see if it's true."

She humored him. "See if what's true?"

"See if my dick really that big."

She couldn't stop herself from chuckling. "Yeah, I guess so. Is it really that big? Show me."

Without hesitation, the short man unbuckled his pants and pushed them midway down his thighs, boxers included. That almost wasn't far enough to make it past his piece, which was more *bizarre* than impressive. He easily surpassed the desired length for a porn star, and he wasn't even erect. As tense as the moment was, the woman couldn't snatch her eyes away from the monstrosity between his legs.

The man's smile broadened. "Yeah, I knew that's what you wanted. Why don't you put that gun down, and let me show you what it do. I'll let bygones be bygones, and you can walk up outta here, if you let me fuck the shit outta yo lil' ass. You gon' be walking bowlegged, but at least you'll be alive."

The woman snorted slightly. Her expression did not change as she lowered her weapon. Midway down, all three men were shocked by the loud report.

BLAK!

Without taking time to properly aim, the woman wasn't sure if her shot was true. But the short man's hands snapped to whatever was left of his dick, and she knew she'd hit her target. A scream caught in his throat, and he was completely silent as he fell to the floor.

In the gasp of silence and absolute horror, the woman glanced down at the man and spoke through the thin veil of gun smoke rising from her pistol. "Guess you ain't fucking the shit outta nobody no more."

The veins stood out on the face of the dickless man, who gasped and moaned, still unable to speak. The shifty man hadn't spoken either. The threat he posed hadn't increased or decreased in the past few moments, but the woman raised her weapon in his direction and ended him with two quick ones to the face.

BLAK!-BLAK!

Just in case.

He was shifty, after all…

The shifty man dropped suddenly and awkwardly, as if a prize fighter had delivered a mean one straight to the chin.

The lone man left standing watched the scene unfold in abject disbelief. He may have pissed himself when she swung the weapon towards him and said, "I told you to–"

"Bitch shot me in the dick," the man on the floor grunted. *"Kill that bitch,"* he pleaded. *"I swear to God I'ma kill you, bitch."*

"I told you to take your clothes off," she continued, as if he had never spoken.

Whatever thoughts the uninjured man had about how this scenario might play out had been vanquished. He began to shed his clothing as if a demanding nurse had made the request.

The downed man's eyes remained squeezed shut as he quickly ran through his options and had an existential change of heart. Rather than request someone gun down the demon woman who had taken *everything* from him with a singular bullet, he addressed the evil entity directly.

"Bitch, kill me," he gasped.

Nothing that had occurred since she entered the pool hall – that wasn't quite a pool hall – would be considered unexpected, as far as the woman was concerned, but she was taken aback by this request.

"You want me to kill you?" she asked, her eyes still on the man who was disrobing.

"I don't wanna live like this," the dickless man said, his voice hoarse and barely audible.

"You sure?" she asked. "Maybe you can get somebody to put it back together. Doctors be doing all kinds of crazy shit these days..."

The last man standing was nearly naked by then. He began to pant loudly, his frantic eyes moving from the gunwoman to his friend – who didn't appear to be mortally wounded, but maybe he was.

"Fuck you, bitch, just–"

BLAK!

The half-naked man recoiled and farted. It took his brain a moment to catch up with the quick movement and the fact that the woman had swung the barrel of the gun downwards and shot his friend, rather than him. The dickless man ceased speaking and moving – and living. The woman raised the gun again. Her eyes were as dead as the men on the floor. She cocked her head slightly, and her small nostrils flared.

"Nigga, you ain't naked yet?"

The survivor couldn't stop his tears from spilling as he ripped the remaining garments from his thin frame. If one of his boys was around to witness this, he might have at least tried to keep his cool. But the only witness to this travesty was his tormentor, and for her, he offered no false bravado. The last man to do that ended up losing his dick, and he wanted no parts of that.

CHAPTER 2

AT GUNPOINT, THE naked man did the female triggerman's bidding. He emptied the pockets of his dead comrades and added whatever cash they had to the pile of money the accountant had left on the bar. He hoped the woman wouldn't notice the duffle bags on the floor next to the pool table, but she was as keen as she was murderous. She wanted that too. He thought she'd leave it at that and leave him to his shame and misery.

Instead she told him, "I know it's a safe behind the bar. Open it, and put whatever's in there in that bag."

The naked man wondered how she knew about the safe, but he didn't dare ask. He considered telling her he didn't know the combination. The only man who knew it was the first man she killed. But he didn't risk that either. He slipped behind the bar and dutifully opened the safe. In addition to a few stacks of cash, there was a 9mm inside. Before he contemplated playing hero, the woman stepped around the bar and watched him from a closer vantage point. With the door of the safe open, he doubted if she could see the gun hidden inside, but he was so freaked out, he couldn't rule out the possibility that she had X-ray vision.

He placed everything inside the duffle bag, including the gun.

With two full duffle bags zipped closed and ready for her to snatch and make her getaway, he stood stiffly, doubting if she'd leave a witness behind but hoping against hope that he would be so lucky. She walked back to the other side of the bar and watched him, rather than take the loot.

The next words the thin man spoke slipped past his lips before he could properly vet them. Curiosity had always been one of his most notable characteristics.

"It, it's you, ain't it?"

Her eyes narrowed, and she humored him. "What you mean?"

"You Brionna. It's you, ain't it?" he repeated.

She took a deep breath. With the rise and fall of her chest, the naked man noticed her nipples for the first time, pushing through the thin fabric of her shirt. He knew this wasn't a good time to indulge, but he always had a thing for braless women with perky tits.

"What you know about Brionna?" she asked.

He swallowed. "I just wanna know if you got who you was here for – if it's you. You came for BD?"

Her eyes flashed and then narrowed again. She shook her head. Her gun remained trained on his chest. "No. I'm here for you, Kenyon."

His eyes widened. He couldn't stop a thunderous chill from racking his body. His voice rattled when he spoke.

"*Wha, what? What you mean? How you know my name?*"

"I just told you; you the one I'm here for."

*"Bu, bu, but, but **why**? What I do?"* Kenyon's eyes glistened, as did the rest of his face.

"I don't ask those kind of questions," Asha said.

"Well, who hired you?" he squealed. *"Can you at least tell me that?"*

His whole body trembled. Asha felt compassion for him – but not enough to make her lower her weapon. At this point, she didn't see any harm in telling him who signed his death warrant. She told him, "BD want you dead."

His eyes grew even larger.

*"**BD**? BD told you to kill me?"*

She nodded.

"But, but that's my dog! And that nigga dead! You just killed him!"

This was the first true surprise she encountered since entering the establishment. "What you mean?" she asked, genuinely confused.

"That's that nigga over there," Kenyon said, gesturing behind her.

Asha wasn't foolish enough to turn away from him.

"That's the nigga you shot in the dick!" Kenyon revealed. *"That's my nigga! You killed him!"*

Asha didn't want to believe him, but at this point, she was almost as good as Boom at detecting when someone was lying to her. Even in his state of distress, with his high shrill voice, she knew Kenyon was telling her the truth.

"Well," she said with a sigh. *"That* wasn't in the plan. I wish I would'a known that before I popped that nigga."

Kenyon had a hard time accepting her nonchalance about the matter, but it did open the door for another ending to this nightmare.

He said, "I can't believe my nigga tried to kill me."

She shrugged. "Happens all the time."

He tried to get his breathing under control as he said, "Well, if, since BD dead, that mean you ain't gotta go through with this then, right? You ain't answering to nobody no more."

She considered that. "I don't know," she mused. "I already fucked around and killed my customer. I don't wanna make it worse by not doing my job."

"But ain't nobody gon' know you didn't do the job!" he cried. *"BD the only one who would'a complained!"*

"I guess you right. *If only you didn't know who I was..."*

Kenyon cursed himself for asking her to verify her identity. *"I ain't gon' come after you,"* he bawled. *"I swear to God! Just take this shit and go."*

She shook her head solemnly. "Sorry, Kenyon. It's best if I gon' and take care of this. Boom ain't gon' like it, if I leave a witness behind."

The naked man knew he didn't stand a chance if he tried to hop over the bar and grab the weapon. But if he was going to die either way, he might as well give it a shot.

He barely had time to place his hands on the countertop before she unloaded the rest of her clip.

CHAPTER 3

WHEN SHE ARRIVED at their home on the east side of Overbrook Meadows, Asha pressed the clicker for the garage door and pulled casually into the roomy space. She hadn't noticed her man following her on the darkened streets, but she wasn't surprised to see him round the corner and pull into the driveway, before she had a chance to lower the door. He parked next to her as she moved to the rear of her Charger and popped the trunk. He exited his vehicle and met her there.

Without words, he stared into her eyes for a few moments, his expression unreadable. He wrapped her up in his big arms and squeezed her tightly. She understood every bit of that.

When he released her, he took a step back and looked her up and down, presumably to make sure she was still in one piece. She took that time to take in his appearance. He sported his notorious beard and ballcap. He wore an Adidas track suit that was all black, other than the white stripes on the arms and legs. Even with the jacket zipped up, the muscles in his arms and chest were prominent. She didn't notice the bulge of any concealed weapons, but she knew he was armed to the teeth. He looked every bit like the dark angel of death.

He hefted the duffle bags without questioning them and headed for the back door. Asha closed the trunk and followed him inside. Their kitchen was spacious and modern. The lingering aromas from the fettucine Boom had prepared earlier was welcoming and still tantalizing. The sight of her beautiful home was comforting, but it was the smells that filled her with a true sense of relief. Despite the horrible things she and her man did on what felt like a daily basis, she had made it home again. She knew she couldn't thank God for the grace she'd been afforded, but she hadn't completely lost her spirituality and could not give praise to Beelzebub, either.

Boom continued to the den and deposited the bags near the sofa. When Asha entered the room, he turned and continued to stare at her, still silent and brooding, like a tiger contemplating the best moment to strike.

She told him, "I didn't know you were following me. You been on my tail the whole time?"

He nodded and said, "If you was on yo job, you woulda known I was following you."

"That's not fair. You go to extreme lengths to make sure no one knows you're on their ass."

"Yeah, and I taught you everything I know. You, of all people, should know when I'm on yo ass."

He took a heavy seat, as if exhausted from a hard day's work.

She came and stood before him, rather than sit down.

She watched him for a few seconds before asking, "You mad at me because I didn't know you were following me, or is it something else?"

He shook his head slightly and sighed. "I ain't mad at you," he said finally. He took off his cap and placed it on the cushion next to him. He rubbed the top of his head with a large palm. "I'm just stressed out. Do you know how hard it was for me to sit out there and listen to them gunshots without knowing who was getting shot? It took everything I had to not run up in there."

"That was supposed to be my solo mission."

"It was. I didn't come in there, did I?"

"But it's not really solo, if I got backup…"

"You saying you don't want backup? That's part of being on a team."

"No, I'm not saying that."

"Trust me," he said, "it's good to have somebody looking out for you."

"I know." She stepped between his legs and dropped to her knees. She leaned forward and embraced him again. With her head resting on his chest, she said, "And I know how hard it was for you to hear those gunshots and not come in. That means you trusted me. You knew I was in there handling my business."

"You got blood on yo shirt," he said. She knew he couldn't see it at the moment, and she also knew he would question her about it.

"You got too close to somebody," he deduced. "Using a pistol, you woulda had to be within ten feet to get blood on you."

Asha didn't want to tell him that at one point she'd been close enough to press the barrel of her gun against the short man's face. But she didn't deny the obvious.

She pulled back and looked him in the eyes, her hands resting on his knees. "They was all standing near the door when I went in. One of 'em started talking shit, so I had to make an example out of him."

Boom nodded. "That's good."

"Uh, not really," she said with a roll of her eyes. "Turns out that was *BD*. I fucked around and killed our client."

Boom frowned. "You killed BD?"

"Yeah, but I didn't know who it was when I did it. I didn't find out till later."

She explained how things had played out inside the Pit Stop. Boom listened intently. Asha always felt anxious and exposed when she gave her man a play-by-play of one of her jobs. He had already been critical of her for not realizing she was being followed. Surely he'd find fault in something else she'd done as she carried out her mission. When she was done talking, he surprised her by leaning back on the sofa with a grimace.

"Damn, that's fucked up."

She had a good idea what he was referring to, but she asked him, "What part?"

"What you mean, *What part*? You shot that nigga in the dick! You ain't never supposed to shoot a nigga in the dick, no matter how mad he make you. I done tortured a lot of people in my lifetime, but I ain't never did nothing to they dick. I see why that nigga wanted you to gone and take him out."

"What? Are you serious? You'd wanna *die* if something happened to yo dick?"

"Shit, quit playing. Yo ass would prolly wanna die too, if something happened to *my* dick."

Asha laughed at that. "No, I wouldn't. I love you for what's in here," she said, rubbing his chest. "As long as you keep eating this pussy, I'd be alright."

"Yeah, right."

"I can't believe you're more focused on where I shot this dude instead of the fact that I killed our customer. Did you know he was gonna be in there? I feel so *stupid*."

"Hey, it's not your fault. That nigga shouldn't have been hanging around some nigga he green-lighted. That's on him. He knew somebody was coming to take Kenyon out. I guess if I was the one who did the job," he relented, "I would've known it was him and let him make it. But don't feel too bad about it. Maybe I should've told you BD be bragging on his dick. You would've known it was him when he started that shit. That's why they call 'em BD."

Asha frowned. "Don't tell me..."

He told her anyway. "*Big Dick,* that's what BD stand for. I'm pretty sure he gave hisself that name. Ain't no real nigga finna call another nigga *Big Dick.* But that nigga was respected enough to get people to call him BD."

"And he wasn't lying about that," Asha said but stopped short of fully praising another man's Johnson. "What will the streets have to say about this?" she wondered.

"Nothing," Boom said with a shrug. "BD was the only one who knew there was a hit on Kenyon. Everybody will think somebody robbed and bodied them niggas. Story won't go no further than that. The only thing we'll miss out on is the second half of the payment for taking out Kenyon.

You know BD only paid half up front. But I'm guessing whatever you brought back in them bags is enough to cover that..."

"I'm pretty sure it is. It's some dope in there too. I know you don't like messing with that..."

"It's okay. I can move it. Why don't you go take a shower," he said, "and I'll check out what you got."

"Okay," she said, rising to her feet.

As she exited the room, Boom told her, "Make sure you–"

"I know. Put everything I got on in a trash bag, so you can get rid of it."

"So you do pay attention *sometimes*," he said as he leaned forward and dragged one of the bags between his legs.

Asha shot him a smirk, but he was focused on other things and didn't notice.

CHAPTER 4

SHE DIDN'T BOTHER putting anything on when she left the bathroom, except a spritz of Moonlight Path on her neck, chest and belly.

On the way back to the den, she encountered Boom in the kitchen. He stood at the sink washing his hands. She knew he must have been done counting the money and wanted to get the *filth* off his hands. Boom wasn't a full-on germaphobe, but he was quick to tell her, *Money nasty as hell. People put it in all kinds of places –their shoes, bras, panties. You don't know where that shit been.*

He watched her as she walked past him. Before she disappeared into the den, she looked back and caught his eyes glued to her ass.

"What?" she said, her eyes sultry and flirtatious.

"What you mean, *what*?" he said. "You know what I'm staring at."

"You must see something you like."

"I'd have to be blind not to..."

In the den, the duffle bags lay empty next to the coffee table. On the tabletop, there were six, neat stacks of cash. Five were roughly the same size. The sixth was notably smaller. Next to the money were large Ziplock bags that contained what appeared to be cocaine, but it may have been heroin. Boom approached from behind and stood next to her. Together they surveyed her haul.

"I didn't think I had that much," she told him. "It didn't seem like a lot when Kenyon was loading the bags."

Boom placed a hand on her waist, but it quickly moved to her ass. He palmed her left cheek, rubbing tenderly.

"Yeah, you did good, babe. I wasn't feeling the jack game at first, but now I wish I'd been doing it all along. Don't make no sense to leave a dead man in a house full of dope and money. I don't know what the hell I was thinking."

"You counted it?" she asked. "How close are we to our goal?"

Their *goal* was five million in laundered cash. Boom thought that would be enough for them to retire from the murder game, buy a home somewhere warm, settle down and start a business that would sustain them financially, well into their golden years. Asha was interested in opening a chain of salons. Boom wanted to try his hand at a trucking company.

"The bigger stacks are 50 G's," he said. "That's two-fifty and some change – plus whatever I get for the coke. If we go the slow route, I can find somebody to rock it up and move it like that. If you want it gone in the next couple of days, I might be able to get fifty or sixty wholesale. I had promised BD I'd give him half of what I recovered – another reason why I ain't too upset about you taking him out. It feels a lot better to keep it all."

"As far as our goal," he said, "after the wash, we should still be looking at three hundred thousand, especially if we rock up the dope. That should put us close to three mil', if not over."

Asha's eyes twinkled. Three hundred thousand for one job, and she'd done it all by herself. She took a deep breath and blew it out slowly. She wished she could count down the remaining jobs before they hit that mark, but it was impossible. A regular hit only paid twenty to thirty thousand. They'd been bringing in more since they added robbery to their repertoire, but they never knew how much money a soon-to-be-deceased victim had available for the taking.

"I know you ready to be done with this," Boom said, reading her mind.

She turned to face him. "Yeah, I am. Ain't you?"

He nodded. "Yeah, especially nowadays. The harder I fall for you, the harder it is to send you out there. Tonight – I knew you'd be okay, but that shit was nerve-racking. I ain't used to worrying about nobody like this."

Asha smiled as she stared into his eyes. Her man would never be a hopeless romantic, but sometimes his words were so endearing, he made her heart sigh. Other parts of her responded as well.

"Come here," she said. She took his hand and led him back to the sofa. "Lemme see *your* BD."

He chuckled. "I know you ain't trying to get me in the mood talking about some dick you shot off."

"Oh, you not gon' get in the mood?" she teased. She took a seat on the sofa and gripped the waist of his pants to pull him between her legs. She pulled the track pants down his thighs and saw that he was already responding to her. She leaned forward and licked and kissed his dick but did not take him into her mouth until he was halfway erect. Once he slid into her warm wetness, she didn't have to suck for very long before he was rock hard.

"*Damn, baby*," he groaned. "I swear you the best at everything you do."

He reached with both hands and placed them on the side and back of her head. She hoped he would fuck her face, but he was content with letting her control the action. He shuddered a moment before his dick throbbed in her mouth, and she tasted his precum.

She backed away for a moment and asked him, "You wanna cum in my mouth?"

His dick continued to pulsate against her lips, but he shook his head. She wondered where he found the willpower to lie to her when his eyes and every other part of his body was screaming the truth.

She stood and switched places with him. When he sat on the sofa, she knelt and pulled his pants the rest of the way down his legs. She knew he didn't like to make love with his ankles hindered, so she removed his shoes and took his pants off completely. In the meantime, he freed himself of his jacket and tee shirt. She wanted to taste his cum so badly, the longing was near desperation, but she straddled him instead. She was beyond wet, but Boom still stretched her walls as she eased down onto him.

With a hand on both of his strong shoulders, she began to ride him. Boom reached and grabbed an ass cheek in each hand. His grip tightened with the heightening of his pleasure. She leaned down and kissed him softly, her movements slow and intense.

"I love you, Enzo."

Boom never left her hanging when she professed her adoration, but he was such a dark and menacing phenomenon, it made her pussy shudder when he returned the affection.

"I love you, too."

She came hard and fast, coating his dick with her essence.

He waited until her throes of passion subsided before he stood, lifting her, his dick still balls deep. He deposited her gingerly on the floor, next to their ill-gotten gains, and hiked her legs up, until her knees were nearly even with his shoulders. Asha's eyes fluttered open, and her throat caught when she saw the beastly demanding in his eyes.

He stroked her slowly, at first.

A few minutes later, he began to pound hard and fast, like he was digging for gold.

PART ONE
DOG MAN

CHAPTER 5

AFTER TWO WEEKS, the uproar over the murder and robbery of BD and his cohorts had mostly died down. As Boom predicted, neither the streets nor the police could offer a cause for the murders, other than what appeared to be obvious: An unknown assailant had come to take the money and drugs known to be in the Pit Stop. The three men had been killed to eliminate witnesses or because they refused to cooperate.

Most thought BD was the primary target, due to the heinous details about his wounds. No one knew of anyone who would do something so vile. The detectives continued to search for the gunman or possibly gunmen, but as far as the hood was concerned, this was yet another predictable outcome of the dope game.

Case closed.

On Monday, July 5th, most 9-5 clock-punchers were off work to celebrate Independence Day, which was on Sunday this year. Most essential workers were still on the job. Murder for hire was always essential, so Asha and Boom drove to a south side apartment complex that morning to meet with a client.

When they arrived at the apartments, Boom backed into a parking spot and instructed Asha to get into the backseat. They waited for a little over ten minutes for their client to arrive. They didn't speak much in the interim. Boom was on high alert, always wary of a setup. His dark eyes took in everything around them, scrutinizing anything that made the slightest movement.

When a Ford F-150 pulled into a parking spot near them, Asha studied the man who exited the vehicle. He was tall and bald, with a pencil thin moustache and goatee. He wore jeans and a tee shirt. He didn't appear to be armed, but Asha was tasked with watching her man's back, if the client tried something. She knew she wasn't really needed for that, but she appreciated Boom allowing her to tag along. If nothing else, this would prevent her from accidently killing their customer again.

When he approached Boom's SUV, the man eyed her warily through the back window, before climbing in on the passenger side. He looked over his shoulder and asked, "Who's this bitch?" as Boom rolled out of his parking spot. The dark assassin shot him a look that would've made anyone recoil.

"*You better watch yo motherfucking mouth*," Boom growled. "How would you like it if she reach over that seat and strangle the shit outta yo ass with a piano wire?"

Asha didn't have a piano wire, but she could get the job done just as easily with the Sig Sauer resting on her lap. The gun was concealed under a scarf that was out of season, therefore just as conspicuous, but Boom had assured her, "It don't matter if it don't look normal. He shouldn't be looking at you no way."

Eyes wide, the color drained from their client's face. "I, I'm sorry Boom. I didn't mean no disrespect. I'm sorry, Ma'am," he said, shooting Asha a glance. "I don't know you, and I ain't got no right to speak to you like that. I didn't mean nothing by it."

Boom didn't immediately respond. Asha didn't think it was right for him to let the man stew in the uncertainty of whether he might actually get strangled or not. But she appreciated him for defending her honor.

"Whatever," he finally replied. "Let's just get down to business. Who is it you want me to meet up with, and when you want it done?"

The client was certainly ready to move past his gaffe. "His name is Greg Putney, but he go by *Dog Man*. You'll find out why when you get close to him. You should watch out for them dogs. That's his first line of defense."

"*Dogs*?" Boom said. "What kind of dogs?"

"I think he mostly keep rotts, but he might have some pits too."

"What you mean *some*? He got, like, a *gang* of 'em?"

"He got more than two or three, and they ain't just for show. They'll tear yo hand off, if you get too close to 'em."

Boom wasn't concerned about anyone's dogs, but he used the information to push his price up. "That's gon' cost you *thirty*, if I have to get past his dogs to get to him."

"That's fine," the client said without hesitation.

"You got an address and know where he be hanging at?" Boom asked.

"I got his address, but he don't hang out too much, not like he used to. Ever since he got on that meth, that nigga mostly be at home skitzing. That's another thing you gotta watch out for. That nigga skittish than a motherfucker. It ain't gon' be easy to sneak up on him."

Boom nodded. "What's the address?"

The man gave him an address not far from where they had picked him up.

"Lemme see his picture," Boom said.

The man reached into his pocket. Asha couldn't tell what he was reaching for, but his sudden movement made her pull her pistol from beneath the scarf. She pointed it at the center of the back seat.

A moment later, the client said, "I got a pic of him on my phone. Hold up a sec..."

Asha returned her weapon to her lap and pulled the scarf back over it. She looked up in the rearview mirror and met Boom's eyes. She couldn't tell what he was thinking, before his attention returned to their client.

"Here he is," the man said. "Want me to send you this picture?"

"Hell naw," Boom said. He looked down and studied the phone before returning his eyes to the road. "Alright. I got it."

"He owe me half a mil'," the client said. "He should have it on him. I know it's in his house somewhere. You can get that for me?"

"Looking for money ain't what I do," Boom lied. "I ain't trying to stick around after I meet somebody. But if I do it, my finder's fee is *half*."

The man went quiet. Asha knew he wasn't happy to hear that. After a few seconds he sighed. "Alright. I guess half is better than not getting none of my money."

"Damn right it's better than none," Boom said. "A quarter mil's way better than none."

"Yeah, you right about that," the client said, in better spirits.

"When you want this done?"

"I wanted my money *yesterday*. If I can get it tomorrow, that would make me happy. But I understand if you can't pull it off that fast."

"I'll see what I can do," Boom replied.

Asha hadn't realized he'd timed their ride to end so quickly, but Boom turned into the apartment complex less than a minute later. He returned their client to his truck and drove away at the same slow pace.

"What you think about this one?" Asha asked from the backseat.

Boom gave it some thought before replying. "Addicts are unpredictable, but I'd rather go after a skitzing meth-head than a strapped-up goon any day."

"We gon' try to take care of this tonight?"

"*We*?"

"We a team, ain't we?"

He sighed slightly. "You can roll as backup, but I'm taking point on this one." Before she could complain, he added, "I know you know what you doing, but I ain't trained you on how to deal with no dogs."

Asha couldn't deny that was the case, so she didn't offer a rebuttal.

CHAPTER 6

THEY DECIDED TO try to give it a go that night.

Boom located the target and surveilled the property at two a.m. After his assessment, he called Asha using his Bluetooth earbuds. From her location, she answered using the same device.

"Hey," she said.

"You in place?" Boom asked. He sat, clad in black, in the dark confines of his SUV, parked a few houses down from the mark. The front of his vehicle faced the target's house.

"Yeah, I'm here," Asha told him.

Boom didn't hear any traffic on her end of the line. Her voice was slightly muffled due to her helmet.

"What it look like?" she asked him.

"He's here," Boom reported. "I'm pretty sure it's him. This nigga been bouncing around the house, like he know somebody coming for him. He been checking all the windows. He ain't settled down in the past thirty minutes."

"You think somebody tipped him off?"

"Naw. I think he full of that shit, like the man said. That meth give you paranoia."

"You got eyes on him now?"

"Yup," Boom said. "Got my binoculars. He at the front door now, prolly looking through the peephole."

Boom's binoculars were equipped with night vision and thermal imaging technology. Through their lenses, the scene before him was well lit, tinted green. The infrared allowed him to see through Dog Man's walls and front door. From Boom's perspective, the target appeared as a glowing figure, mostly red.

"You gon' take the shot?" Asha asked. She knew he had the same technology on the scope of his favorite sniper rifle.

"I don't think so," her man replied. "He moving around too much. If I miss, he gon' bolt."

Asha knew Boom was an expert marksman. If he didn't think it was a good shot, she had to take his word for it.

"What about the dogs?" she asked.

"I ain't seen none."

"He said there would be dogs."

"I know. I been looking for 'em. I checked the backyard. Didn't see none there, either."

"You got on the property?"

"No. But I could tell some dogs had been back there. I saw some food bowls and some chains. But no dogs. I didn't have my binoculars when I went to the back, so I might have missed them. But I think they woulda started barking, if they was back there."

"You sure they not in the house?"

"I'm sure. The only thing moving in there is him."

"That don't sit right with me."

"Me neither. But I don't always get good intel. Maybe he got rid of his dogs."

"I don't see why he would, especially if he think somebody coming for him."

"Yeah. I was thinking the same."

"I think you should take the shot. If he bolt, I can intercept."

"I'd rather get him in the house, jack him up and find out where the money at. There's a car in the backyard. I saw some tire tracks leading from the driveway. If he take off, I think he'll try to make it to that car. I'm pretty sure I can get to him, before he make it out there."

"You talking about going in through the front or the back?"

"I'm thinking the front. I don't wanna try the back, 'cause I might be wrong about the dogs. Just gotta wait till he move away from the door. He all over the place, but he do got some kind of pattern. After checking the front of the house, he go to the back and start checking them windows for a while."

"I ain't feeling this. You don't know what he got going on in there."

"Why you acting like I ain't never did this before?"

Asha knew he was right. Boom had been known to run up in a house full of goons who were both armed and waiting for him. Most recently, he assaulted the home of a thug named OG Ruckus. Not only did Boom manage to kill five armed men inside the house – OG Ruckus included – but he kidnapped the lone survivor when he made his escape.

"Okay," Asha said. "What you need me to do?"

"Just stay in position," Boom told her. "And stay on the line. If shit go left, be ready to intercept."

"Alright, baby. I'm ready. Be careful."

CHAPTER
7

BEFORE EXITING HIS vehicle, Boom traded his ballcap for night vision goggles, which strapped over and around his head. He always had the appearance of a night stalker, but the futuristic gear made him look even more ghastly as he crept quickly and purposefully past the target's neighbors' houses. A few of them had porch lights on. Boom knew his approach might be revealed as he lurked past them. He relied on his timing and the element of surprise.

Dog Man had left the front of the house a few moments before Boom left his SUV. His goggles didn't have infrared visioning, so there was no way to know if the skittish man had returned.

Either way, once he reached the property, it was go time.

Boom announced his arrival by tossing a flashbang grenade through the front window, quickly followed by a smoke bomb. The moment the grenade went off, hopefully blinding and disorientating anyone in the vicinity, he charged the front door and breached the entrance with a thunderous kick next to the doorknob.

BOOMP!

The deadbolt was solid, but the doorframe was not. The splintering of the wood as it was ripped from the frame was lost in the sound of the door crashing into the opposite wall. Boom rushed in right behind it. The living room was filled with smoke. A quick sweep with the weapon he'd chosen for this job, an AR-15, revealed the front room was not occupied. He tossed another smoke bomb down the hallway ahead of him before marching in that direction, his weapon raised, his keen eyes capturing everything.

A sound near the rear of the house caught his attention. It was a sound he was familiar with – locks being unfastened. First the deadbolt, then the doorknob, then the swing bar, in rapid succession. He hurried in that direction but didn't make it in time before the target slipped through the exit. Boom raised his weapon but couldn't get a shot off in time.

Undaunted, he picked up the pace. He reached the back door and put eyes on the target just as Dog Man made it to his car. As Boom raised his weapon again, he first heard and then saw something that put self-preservation a few notches above murder.

What he heard was a high-pitched voice screaming, "_Get him, boys! Get him!_"

What he saw was two monsters explode from Dog Man's Camry the moment he opened the door. The dogs didn't bark or growl as they sprinted to the back door. The rottweilers were huge, dark masses of eyes, claws and teeth. Boom slammed the door closed, just as they crashed into it. They began to bark then. They snarled and scratched the door, fully intending to rip it apart if possible. Beyond them, Boom heard the car start. A moment later, the squeal of tires cut through the night as Dog Man made his escape.

"*He on the move!*" Boom shouted to his partner, who had been listening to his failed attempt silently and anxiously.

Asha's voice was professional and almost calm as she started her motorcycle. "Alright, I'll get him."

The scream of her bike's engine was nearly deafening in his earbuds, but Boom did not disconnect the call. He placed his assault rifle on the countertop and casually reached to his belt, which had more gadgets than Batman's. He selected a remedy for the dogs. He cracked the door slightly and had to use every bit of his strength to keep the dogs from forcing their way inside. Immediately, both savages crammed their muzzles through the opening. Their fangs were as intimidating as they were deadly. The animals snapped and snarled, trying their best to get a chunk of the enemy, who was so close they could almost taste him.

Boom gave them both a full blast of bear spray. The chemicals invaded their mouths, noses and eyes and was instantly incapacitating. The dogs withdrew from the opening, like a turtle retreating into its shell, and stumbled into the darkness, shrieking and howling their discontent.

"*Dammit,*" Boom cursed himself.

"*You alright, baby?*" Asha had to raise her voice to a shout as the force of the wind streaking past her face rendered the Bluetooth almost unusable.

"Yeah," Boom said, doubtful she could hear him.

He closed the door again and locked it before hefting his rifle and turning back towards the kitchen. If his entry into the home didn't rouse suspicion, the racket the dogs were kicking up certainly would. He checked his watch, estimating he had less than three minutes before the first neighbor called the police. In this neighborhood, their response time might buy him another few minutes. He gave himself two minutes to search for the money. He hoped he wouldn't encounter a nosey neighbor on his way out.

It was never his intention to harm an innocent, but no one and nothing would stop him from making it back to his SUV parked down the street.

CHAPTER 8

GREG PUTNEY, AKA Dog Man, realized he'd been right all along. Rather than his one-time business associate, who sported a pencil-thin goatee, Dog Man suspected the FBI was on to him because he opened a bank account with cash last week, depositing two thousand dollars. The feds had used the serial numbers on the bills to trace them back to the dirty dealings he'd been involved in.

For the past week, Dog Man had expected a raid. He expected a SWAT team. He expected an assassin. For the past few nights, he expected a horde of ninjas. On more than one occasion, he had actually seen the ninjas in the trees behind his house. They hid high amongst the leaves, barely moving and barely breathing. They thought he hadn't seen them, but he had.

Dog Man did not believe he was crazy. He did not believe the large amounts of methamphetamine he'd been smoking and recently injecting played a part in any of this. He wasn't delusional. If he was delusional, then why had the FBI just raided his home? He managed to escape, but he wasn't stupid enough to think it was that easy. His wide, panicked eyes checked the side and rearview mirrors as often as he checked the road ahead of him. He saw one of the ninjas following him on a motorcycle.

His face drenched with sweat, he cut another corner and floored it again. The Camry's engine bucked. He squeezed the steering wheel so tightly, his fingertips were numb. His heart raced faster that the pistons under the hood of his car. Dog Man knew that his only hope was to make it to the Trinity River. The ninjas would not pursue him in the water, because water is a ninja's weakness.

Everyone knew that.

Asha was both unaware and unconcerned about the delusions her target was suffering from. Unlike the ravaged mind of a meth-head, her approach to this problem was based on logic and reasoning. The car she was pursuing could no longer move quickly or erratically once she removed the driver from the equation. That was simple math.

She followed him around another corner and drew a pistol from her chest holster. With one hand maintaining control of the bike, she took aim at the back windshield and let off four shots. At least one of them hit its mark. The Camry jerked violently to the right, sideswiped a car parked along the curb and continued forward at a slower pace before hopping a curb and colliding with a streetlamp.

Asha followed him, coming to a stop twenty feet away. She lowered the kickstand but did not kill the engine on her Fireblade SP. The mean machine was identical to another sport bike she totaled on a previous job.

Hearing a lull in the action on her end, Boom asked her, "Everything good?"

"I think I got him," Asha said. She approached the Camry's driver's side at an angle, her weapon drawn. She held the Sig Sauer with both hands, like a police officer.

When she got closer, she saw that the driver was slumped over, almost fully in the passenger seat. He didn't appear to be breathing. With a gloved hand, she opened the door for a closer inspection. The interior of the car was bloody, as was the target. Without leaning into the car, she couldn't tell if she'd got a headshot, but she knew Boom wouldn't leave the body unless he was sure.

"I'ma go to the other side and finish him off."

"A'ight. You ran him down on the street?"

"Yeah."

"You love that damn bike."

"Couldn't have done this without it."

"I think I'ma head out," Boom said. "I couldn't find–"

BLAT! BLAT!

"I didn't find nothing here," he continued, as if a human soul hadn't just been forcibly ejected from its owner.

"If it ain't in the house, that mean it gotta be in this car then, right?" Asha said.

"You see something in there?"

"Not in the front. Hold up a sec."

"Where you at? You need me to meet you?"

"St. Louis and Butler. But I won't be here long. Nothing in the back either," she reported.

"You gon' check the trunk? I don't think he woulda took off without the money."

"Yeah, let me go over here and pop it."

Asha returned to the driver's side and looked for the trunk release near the steering wheel.

"Ain't no witnesses?"

"No. Not yet."

"You need to hurry up. I know you don't wanna give up that bike."

"I ain't giving up this bike."

"If somebody see you, you *are* giving it up. I'm headed back to my car."

"Alright."

Asha reached over the dead man's lap and pressed the button. She barely had time to back out of the car before Dog Man's resourcefulness reared its ugly head again.

"Oh shit!"

Like the first set of dogs, the rottweiler that sprang from the trunk did not make a sound as it rounded the car, spotted its target and attacked. Asha did not have time to vocalize what was going on before the beast was upon her, biting and clawing and snarling now.

***"Asha*!"**

From his end of the line, Boom heard everything clearly. It was the same sound he'd heard when the maneaters were trying to force their way through the back door. The only difference now was the whining, urging insistence was missing from the beast attacking his woman. This dog had made contact with the target and had entered phase two of its training.

Bite.

Bite.

Bite.

Destroy.

***"Asha*!"**

For the next three minutes, Boom drove as frantically and wide-eyed as Dog Man had when he made his getaway. Engaged in what might have been the fight of her life, Asha didn't speak much. Tasked with keeping the sharp, drooling fangs away from her neck, the only thing she said to Boom was, "*I dropped my gun!*" and "*Fuck! This nigga biting me! He got me down!*" Other than that, the prominent sound on the other end of the line was snarling, a symphony of gut-wrenching struggles that twisted Boom's guts in knots. Every gasp and cry from his woman impacted him like a cannonball to the chest.

He was caught up in a whirlwind of rage, grief and panic by the time he turned the last corner and saw the wrecked Camry with its front bumper twisted around the light pole. He jumped from his SUV and ran to the bodies on the ground. At first, all he saw was the dog, lying on its stomach, motionless.

But then he saw his woman's limbs protruding from beneath the animal. A grunt of despair escaped him as he reached for the dog's collar and tossed the 130-pound behemoth aside as easily as he would heft a gallon of milk. Beneath the dog, his woman lie on her back. She hadn't been able to retrieve her pistol, but she had her hunting knife in hand. It was coated with blood. Boom knew she kept the knife in an ankle holster. He had no idea how she managed to retrieve the weapon and defend herself, but the fact that she had was obvious. The dog was dead. He prayed his woman was not.

He knelt to remove her helmet. Asha surprised him by sitting up. She batted his hands away.

"*No, don't take it off,*" she breathed. "*There might be cameras.*"

Her voice was hoarse, but it was not accompanied by the wet, gurgling sound of someone with a neck wound. Boom could not say the same about her hands and arms.

Even in the darkness, he could see that the damage was extensive.

"*Get my gun*," Asha said and tried to make it to her feet. "*Check the trunk.*"

There was so much to come to terms with, Boom struggled to wrap his mind around everything. Not only had Asha survived the attack, but she still had the wherewithal to understand they were still on a job, and there were things that needed to be attended to. Boom was usually the one to provide this level of resolve.

He understood, not for the first time, that his woman was a soldier.

He helped her to her feet and hurried to collect her weapon. As he moved to check the trunk of the Camry, he was surprised to see Asha limping towards her bike. Inside the trunk he found a large, military duffle bag. He hoisted it, without checking the contents, and hurried to catch up with Asha.

"*Where you going? You need to ride with me.*"

"No. I can't leave my bike here."

"*Fuck this bike! I'll come back for it!*"

"*No! It's evidence. I can make it home,*" she panted. "*I'll meet you there. Hurry up.*"

Boom was not okay with any of this, but he knew Asha was telling him right. He took the duffle bag to his SUV and hopped behind the wheel. He caught up with the sport bike as she drove away. He stayed on her tail the whole way home, praying that she wouldn't pass out on the interstate.

CHAPTER 9

ASHA MADE A few questionable lane changes without signaling while Boom followed her home. He feared she'd continue gliding right off the shoulder or into a guardrail while he watched, powerless to do anything about it. But she pulled it together and straightened her bike each time.

When they arrived at their home, Boom left his truck in the driveway and hurried to assist Asha when she pulled into the garage. She fell into his arms when she attempted to get off of her bike. In the brightly lit garage, all he saw was blood, on her helmet, torso, and even her legs. Her arms were fully drenched.

The only saving grace was the leather jacket Asha always wore when she was on her Honda. Even with a cursory inspection, Boom could see that many of the bite marks had not penetrated the leather. He hefted his woman and carried her into their home, as if he was crossing the threshold after their wedding. He bypassed the hard kitchen floor and took her to the living room. He gently placed her on the leather sofa without a care for the bloodstains she would leave there.

When he got her helmet off, he was grateful to see no scars on her beautiful face. There was a deep scratch on her neck, but Asha had done well to keep the dog away from her carotid arteries. Her eyes were half closed. Her eyelids fluttered as she looked up at him.

"*Did you get the money?*" she asked, her voice little more than a croak. "*Did you check his trunk?*"

Boom's heart bled for her. "Don't worry about that right now. Let me get this jacket off and see how bad you're hurt. I think we need to go see Doc."

"Just tell me if you got the money," she said.

Boom did not agree with her priorities at the moment, but if she could have the strength to put the job ahead of her injuries, he was strong enough to get through this as well.

"I got a bag out the trunk," he said. "I don't know what's in it. Here, I'ma lift you up, to get this jacket off."

She winced as he sat her up. She cried out in pain when he worked on freeing her left arm from the sleeve of the jacket. He gritted his teeth, feeling every bit of her agony. With one arm free, he saw that she had a few puncture marks on that arm, but as expected, the jacket prevented most of the bites from getting through. Instead, her arm was dotted with bruises.

When he got the jacket off completely, he saw that the other arm was in similar condition. The worst damage was to her hands. Asha wore gloves during the job, but the material wasn't as durable as her jacket. Her left hand was worse for wear. Boom knew she'd been busy stabbing the canine with her right hand. The left was all she had for defense.

"I grabbed his collar," she said, "trying to hold him back as best I could. But he got a couple of bites on me."

That was an understatement. Boom could tell she needed stiches to close up a few of the wounds.

"I gotta take you to see Doc," he said again. "Let me go get some gauze to wrap this up and stop the bleeding before we leave."

"What about the bag?" she asked.

"Don't worry about–"

"*I am worried about that.*"

Boom didn't know where she found the force to harden her eyes at him, but she did.

"After what I been through," she said, "I need to know if we got what we was looking for – if we closer to retirement."

He stared at her for a moment and then sighed. "Can I at least get you wrapped up first?"

She brought her hands into her lap and cradled them there. She shook her head. "Go get the bag. I'll be alright 'til you get back."

Boom returned to the driveway and dragged the duffle bag from the backseat. He brought it back to the living room and deposited it at the warrior's feet, so she could see her spoils of war. Asha was ashen, her lips parched. She sat up and leaned forward to peer into the bag as Boom unzipped it.

She said, "I swear, if it's another dog in there..."

Boom looked up at her. It made him feel better to see that she still had a sense of humor, but he didn't crack a smile. Inside the bag was a number of stacked and wrapped bills. Without counting it, he couldn't be sure, but Boom had come into contact with enough money to know what half a million looked and felt like.

Judging by the weight alone, he told her, "I think it's all here."

"Half of it's ours," Asha said.

"We should keep all of it, after what we went through to get it."

He wasn't serious, but Asha shot that down.

"No. We gotta keep our integrity. It only take one nigga to talk shit about us, to make our money start drying up. We too close to the finish line to let that happen."

He nodded. "I know. Wait here, I'ma go get some bandages."

CHAPTER
10

TWENTY MINUTES LATER, they were on the road again, this time in a black-on-black Charger. It was nearly four a.m. The streets were mostly deserted.

"How you holding up?" Boom asked his woman, who was awake but not necessarily alert in the passenger seat.

"I'm okay," she said, her eyelids drooping. "Where we going?" she asked, noticing they were leaving the city limits, away from the larger hospitals.

"I told you, we're going to see Doc."

"I know. I thought you were taking me to a doctor."

"He is a doctor. A *vet*, but that's still a doctor."

Asha looked over at him. Boom was without any of his disguises. His face was clean-shaven, his hair cut low. He was still clad in all black.

"*A vet*?" she said. "You taking me to a vet?"

"You don't think a vet can take care of you?"

"Yeah, I guess he could, but..." She frowned. There were so many questions. "How you even meet up with a vet at this time of night? Why they even open?"

"I've known Doc for a long time," he informed her. "I don't get injured too often, but when I do, I go see him. You know I can't go to the hospital, after I done shot some people up. If not the police, the hospital's one of the easiest places for an opp to get a hold of you. You remember what happed to Big Hooch…"

Asha found it interesting that he referred to the silenced gangster as if he didn't have anything to do with the lethal concoction injected into Hooch's IV. She didn't accompany Boom on that job, but he later explained how easy it was to slip into Big Hooch's hospital room.

"Doc has an animal hospital in Cedar Hill," Boom said. "He usually take big animals – horses and cows and shit – but they service dogs and cats too. His clinic ain't open, but he'll meet with me damn near any time of night. He ain't cheap, but it's worth it to keep us out the hospital."

Asha nodded. She never imagined she'd one day receive medical care from a veterinarian, but since she'd been with Boom, stranger things had happened.

"Plus I'm worried about all that DNA you left with Dog Man," he said. "A scene like that, I woulda got my gas and set all that shit on fire. But we didn't have time. For a murder, you know they'll keep any unknown DNA on file. They'll be trying to match your blood with somebody for years. Anyone who gets sent to prison automatically get their DNA put in a database and ran against whatever DNA they looking for."

"I guess I'm good then," Asha said, "'cause I ain't never going back to prison. Might have to go head-to-head with a rott, but I ain't getting locked up."

"You ain't going head-to-head with no more rotts either."

Asha didn't tell Boom he was making a promise he couldn't keep. Likewise, he didn't tell her she was doing the same.

CHAPTER
11

IT WAS AFTER four when they arrived at the Central Animal Hospital. There was only one car in the parking lot of the large building, a newer model Mercedes. Boom parked next to it but remained in his vehicle. Someone stepped out of the Benz and approached the Charger on the driver's side. Boom rolled down his window to greet him.

Doc didn't look like a doctor – or a veterinarian for that matter. As he peered into the window, Asha saw that he was middle aged, maybe in his early fifties. He wore jeans and a tee shirt and toted a thermos. He was clean shaven, with long hair that was balding up top. The rest was pulled back away from his face.

He took a sip of what Asha assumed was coffee and told Boom, "Good morning." He didn't appear upset about being roused at such an early hour. Asha knew the power of the almighty dollar was one hell of an incentive.

"Morning," Boom told him. "Thanks for coming."

The man nodded. "This her?" He looked past Boom and tried to get a look at Asha, but without the dome lights on, the interior of the Charger was mostly shadows.

Boom nodded.

"Heard you had a run in with a bad dog," the vet said. "Mind if I get a look at your arms?"

Asha raised her arms, which were wrapped from her hands up to her elbows.

"I didn't put the bandages on too tight," Boom told him. "I knew you'd take 'em off, and I didn't want it to hurt."

"Looks like you did a good job," Doc said. "I can't tell how much help you'll need from me till I get a good look at 'em." He checked his watch. "My first employee will be here at seven. We gotta make this quick. Follow me around back."

He left them and returned to his vehicle. He backed out of his spot and didn't travel far before stopping at a fence on the side of the building. Boom came to a stop right behind him. The vet left his car and used a key to unlock the gate. He pulled it open, wide enough to accommodate their vehicles, before returning to the Mercedes and continuing his drive.

Behind the main building, Asha saw four more buildings that were smaller, but still large enough to accommodate farm livestock. The Mercedes came to a stop again near the back entrance of the main building. Doc left his car and approached the door, shuffling through his keychain again.

Boom parked next to him and killed the engine. "Don't try to get out by yourself," he told Asha as he exited the vehicle. "Let me help you."

Asha felt she was fully capable of exiting the car on her own, but she didn't thwart Boom's attempt to care for her.

Inside the clinic, the vet led them to an exam room and turned on the lights. Asha saw a few chairs inside and an exam table that was large enough to accommodate a Great Dane. She found the exam table comfortable, if not a little unnerving, when the vet asked her to, "Take a seat."

While he went to the sink to wash his hands and pull on a pair of latex gloves, Asha took in her surroundings. The posters of animals on the walls did not instill her with confidence, but she knew that suturing wounds was a standard procedure that should be universal across different species. More importantly, she knew Boom wouldn't have brought her here if he didn't trust this man.

When he was done, the vet approached the table and said, "Okay, let's have a look."

Rather than remain standing near the door, Boom came and stood by the man's side. Doc carefully removed the bandages, apologizing each time Asha grimaced from the pain.

"Sorry. I'm trying to be careful."

"It's my fault," Boom interjected. "I shouldn't have wrapped it so tight."

"No, no," the other man said. "You did good. Looks like she was bleeding pretty bad. If she bled to death on your way here, wouldn't be anything I could do at that point..."

When he had her hands and arms fully exposed, he took his time to study them. He pursed his lips and narrowed his eyes as he took in all of her wounds. At one point, he whistled and turned her arm over.

"Yeah, this is pretty bad." He let go of her and said, "Can you wiggle your fingers?"

She nodded and showed him that she could.

"Can you make a fist and swirl your wrist around?"

She could do that too.

"What about this hand?" he asked, referring to her left.

Asha repeated the same motions with that hand. Making the fist was difficult, but she managed.

The vet nodded. He examined her left hand again. "Well, the good thing is there doesn't appear to be any broken bones," he said to Boom. "It's too early to tell about nerve damage, but her range of motion looks good. There's two bites on her left hand that need stitches. The rest will close up pretty good with a butterfly bandage. The bruises will hurt for as long as the cuts, and they will probably start to swell. You see these are already starting to swell over here."

Asha wondered why the man was talking to Boom, rather than the patient. She wondered if he had been working with animals for so long, it was hard to break the habit.

"Other than that," he continued, "with any animal bite, we have to worry about infection. If this wasn't a wild animal, we shouldn't have to worry about rabies. But there's no treatment if you get it, so you may want to get some shots, just in case. Problem with the shots is they're painful. I have to inject them near the area where she was bitten. The rest go in her shoulder. After the first batch, she'd have to get three more shots in the next 14 days. Like I said, if it wasn't a wild animal, I doubt if the dog that bit her had rabies, but better safe than sorry."

"The dog that bit her didn't have rabies," Boom said.

"We don't know that," Asha countered.

"Any chance you can bring the animal here for me to test it?" Doc wanted to know.

Boom shook his head.

"I think we should get the shots," Asha said. "Better safe than sorry."

Boom looked her in the eyes and sighed. He nodded. "Alright."

"Good," Doc said. "She's gonna need some antibiotics too. I have to clean these wounds and prep you for sutures," he said, speaking to Asha now. "Before I clean them, I'm gonna give you a local anesthetic. It's lidocaine. I'll administer it with more injections. It'll be painful, but once it kicks in, you won't feel anything. When I'm done with everything, I'll give you more pain meds to take with you."

"You got *human* drugs in here?" Asha had to ask. She looked around the exam room again, her eyes doubtful.

Doc grinned. "I keep enough *human* drugs around for emergencies, special customers. I never know when someone like Boom might call me at three o'clock in the morning..."

CHAPTER
12

WHEN THEY MADE it home again, the sun was beginning to peak over the eastern horizon. Boom helped Asha to the bathroom and ran a bath for her. He made sure to keep her arms elevated when she got in the tub. When she settled into the warm water, he washed her slowly and carefully. Asha lie back against the tub and closed her eyes, her head resting on the edge. Boom stopped bathing her long enough to get a soft towel to rest her head on. When he resumed, the sensations he provided her felt so good, she never wanted to leave the tub. But he drained the water fifteen minutes later and asked, "You sleep?"

She shook her head slightly. Without opening her eyes, she said, "No."

"I know you tired. Let me get you dried off and into bed."

After tending to his woman, Boom bathed himself and joined her on their soft mattress. Asha usually slept on her side, but out of deference to her arms, she remained on her back that night. Before taking his shower, Boom had pulled the sheets up to her shoulders. She was in the same position, fast asleep when he returned. Before lying next to her, he marveled at her strength and beauty.

He remembered the first day he met her. Fresh off her job as an awning installer, Asha was dusty and tomboyish. Her demeanor had matched her appearance, so much so, Boom recalled asking if she was gay. He smiled at the memory. At that moment, almost a year and a half ago, if someone had wagered he and Asha would one day find themselves in this current moment, Boom would've bet his life savings against it – which was why he'd never been a gambling man, especially when it came to something as unpredictable as the future.

He turned off the bathroom lights, which, thanks to their dark curtains, effectively darkened the bedroom. He crawled into bed next to his woman. He tried not to rouse her, didn't think he had, but he felt her head roll in his direction a few moments later. He looked her way and could barely make out the whites of her eyes in the darkness.

"I love you, Enzo."

He sat up on one elbow. Beneath the sheets, he reached for her. He expected to feel her warm belly but came in contact with her bandaged arms instead. This was not surprising, but it served as a painful reminder of the horrible night they'd experienced. He leaned towards her and kissed the corner of her mouth.

"I love you, too. Get some rest."

He lie back and settled into his pillow. He was surprised to feel her hand move towards him. He frowned in the darkness when her bandaged hand found his dick and remained there. He reached for her hand when she tried to wrap it around his manhood.

"Baby, what you doing?" he asked, looking her way again.

"I thought you wanted to make love..."

Boom knew Doc had given her narcotic-strength pain meds to take home, but he hadn't expected her to lose her senses.

He frowned. "I didn't say that. Why would I? You ain't in no condition."

"Making love after a job makes me feel better," she said, revealing that she hadn't lost her senses at all.

Boom was not swayed.

"No, babe. I don't think that's a good idea."

"You can get on top. I promise not to do anything with my hands."

Her voice was so soft and sweet, Boom actually considered it. But he shook his head.

"No, baby. I'm not feeling that. Get some rest."

He sighed and closed his eyes, listening to the quietness of their home. He was doubtful he'd get any sleep, but that was just as well. He preferred to remain alert, in case Asha needed anything. The next sound he heard made him roll towards her again. The sniffle was slight, but it was discernable. Frowning again, he reached and brushed the side of her face with delicate fingers. He was surprised to find it moist.

His brow furrowed with astonishment. This woman had been attacked by a vicious dog. She'd been poked and prodded by a veterinarian. Never once, throughout the whole ordeal, had she shed a tear. But the prospect of not making love to him was powerful enough to make her cry.

Without words, he continued rolling towards her until he was in the position she desired. He made sure to support his upper body with his forearms and avoid contact with her hands and arms. Her eyes remained closed as she spread and raised her legs for him. Under the circumstances, Boom did not think he would become aroused, but the position and his deep love for her overrode his need to keep her safe. His erection was born more out of compassion than desire. Or maybe this selfless act was another component of the care he needed to provide for her.

He found her sweet opening as moist and inviting as it always was. She sucked air between her teeth as he penetrated her. Boom wasn't sure if he'd inadvertently brushed her arm or if she was responding to his size, but he knew what her response would be if he did not proceed.

It did not take long before she voiced her pleasure both vocally and biologically. Boom couldn't help but cum at the same time. When he withdrew and reclined on his pillow again, spent yet exhilarated, he realized he'd needed their lovemaking as much as she had. He had spent so much of his life fully in charge of all situations. It felt good to occasionally relinquish control to a soulmate who oftentimes knew best.

PART TWO
AN OLD FACE

CHAPTER 13

TWO WEEKS LATER, Asha was on the mend. With her stitches out and the bruises on her arms mostly gone, she considered herself fully healed. She'd even gotten the remainder of her rabies shots. Boom had been pampering her ever since the dog attack, and he thought she should take it easy for a little while longer.

So when he prepared to head out one afternoon to meet with a new client, he told her, "I think you should sit this one out."

Asha stood in the bathroom watching him as he dressed in the closet. She might have taken his advice until she saw him strap on *two* ankle holsters, stuffing a small pistol in one and a knife in the other.

"Why you want me to sit this one out?" she asked. "Who you meeting that's making you feel like you need so much protection?"

"It's somebody you know," he said, pulling a tee shirt over his head. "But if I tell you his name, you gon' start tripping."

"What's his name?" she asked, hand on her hip, ready to start tripping.

Boom looked her way and rolled his eyes. He said, "Solomon."

Asha didn't think she'd heard him right. "*Solomon?* You mean *Solomon*, like KD's brother?"

Boom nodded. "Yup."

Asha's mouth fell open. "You can't be serious."

"I am. And I know what you thinking. But I think this is on the up and up."

Asha was incredulous. "Solomon wants to hire you after what you did to his brother – and his father?"

"Johnny wasn't Solomon's father," Boom corrected her. "He was KD's father. They got different dads."

That didn't make her feel any better. Asha shook her head in wonderment. "I can't believe you even serious right now…"

Asha first met Boom shortly after he took out an upper-level dealer named King David, aka KD. After the murder, someone hired a couple of hitters to come after Boom, to avenge KD's death. Asha got caught up in the plot by way of association. She and Boom took out the hitters and then set out to find the person who hired them. After a little detective work, they narrowed the suspects down to three people: Solomon, KD's son, Cole, and KD's father, Johnny.

Asha and Boom interrogated Solomon and Cole before they discovered Johnny was the true culprit. The older man made his last stand with a mess of pipe bombs strapped under his wheelchair. Asha and Boom made sure they were a safe distance away when the bombs exploded, killing only Johnny.

As for Solomon, his interrogation was one of the most gut-wrenching Asha had been party to. She was tasked with threatening the man's daughter, until Boom was satisfied Solomon had told them all he knew. Asha would never forget sitting in the backseat of Solomon's car in the parking lot of a McDonald's. Solomon's daughter had sat next to her, oblivious to what was transpiring at first, but later crying and deciding she didn't want to get ice cream after all. Despite the resilience of children, Asha had often wondered if the little girl would ever enjoy daddy-daughter time again.

"Do I really need to tell you it would be crazy to meet with that man?" Asha asked.

Boom was still in the closet, selecting a pair of sneakers that matched his outfit.

"I know what I'm doing," he replied gruffly. "That nigga know what'll happen if he try something. He ain't stupid."

"*But why take the chance?*"

"'Cause next to Mr. Brown, it's only a handful of real ballers left. Solomon is one of 'em. I don't know who he want me to take out, but it's gon' be some good money involved. I can't pass that up."

Mr. Brown had been another victim of Asha and Boom's murder spree. Asha had taken him out personally, after he sent goons to threaten her family.

"If you serious about meeting him, I'm going," she decided. "You don't know what type of shit that nigga on."

"I'm pretty sure I'm right about this, but I ain't finna argue with you," Boom said. "I'm leaving in fifteen minutes. If you going, be ready by then."

CHAPTER 14

BOOM HAD MADE plans to meet Solomon at one of his safe houses. Asha knew the home well, even though she'd only been there twice, and that was when she first met the bearded menace. Pulling into the driveway brought back a lot of memories, most of them unpleasant. Asha knew that Boom had gotten the garage door repaired, but she'd never seen the finished product. The last time she saw the old door, Boom had plowed directly into it – on purpose – as they fled a hitman duo named Ben and Jerry. Jerry was the first man Asha murdered under Boom's tutelage. Since then, she'd honestly lost count of how many bodies she'd dropped.

When Boom parked and killed the engine, Asha gave him a sideways glance as he lowered the garage door.

"What?" he said.

She said, "You must not trust Solomon *that* much, if you meeting him here."

"I trust him not to try to kill me," Boom explained. "That don't mean I'm taking chances with him possibly working for the feds. I don't know that nigga like *that*. I don't know what type of shit he on."

Asha shook her head with a roll of her eyes.

Boom gave her a smirk. "Just play yo part, and we'll be alright."

"Oh, I'm definitely gon' play my part, prolly a lot better than you want me to."

"Don't scare this nigga off," Boom warned.

Asha made no promises.

Twenty minutes later, Boom had everything set up and ready for their visitor. When a tall figure climbed the porch, Boom opened the door before he had a chance to knock.

Upon coming face to face with the man he'd last seen with a gun trained on him – the bearded monster who threatened his daughter and gave her nightmares for weeks – an awkward chill rolled down Solomon's frame. He quickly shook it off.

"What's up?" he said.

Boom expressed no guilt for what he had done to this man's daughter, his brother or his brother's father. He mean-mugged his guest as if Solomon was the one ripping branches off *his* family tree.

After putting the fear of God into him, with just his eyes, he told him, "Come on."

Solomon casually entered the home. Boom closed and locked the door behind him.

Their new client, or possibly next victim, was handsome, even in his state of uncertainty. Solomon wore a full beard, shaved low. His hair was short, his skin caramel.

"What's up?" Solomon said as he surveyed the room, which had no furniture, other than a lone table in the center.

Sitting atop the table was a gadget that was roughly the size of a laptop, with two sets of wires extending from it. One end was plugged into the wall. The other was connected to some sort of wand.

"Come empty yo pockets on this table," Boom said. He walked away from him and positioned himself on the opposite side of the table. He watched Solomon carefully as the man complied with his instructions.

"What's this?" Solomon asked, referring to the electronic device. "What you got going on in here?"

Boom continued to watch him coldly, rather than respond.

"It's gon' be hard to do business if you don't say nothing–"

CHA-CHIK

Solomon froze, recognizing the sound immediately. He sighed and turned slightly to see who was behind him. He came face to face with the second half of the murder duo. Asha had selected Jamaican garb for this assignment, complete with a rastacap that had a slew of dreadlocks flowing from it, obscuring most of her face. But her appearance was less important than the double barrel shotgun she toted. The business end of the weapon was currently pointed down. Solomon knew she could raise it in an instant.

Seeing the gun, he was reminded that this was Boom's weapon of choice in the early days of his career. Legend had it, you never knew when Boom was on yo ass. By the time you heard that ***BOOM!*** it was too late, he'd accomplished his mission.

Solomon's eyes were filled with disappointment when they returned to the man he'd reached out to for help. "You call me over here to kill me?"

Boom shook his head. "No. Not necessarily. But I'm wondering if that's what you had in mind for me."

"I ain't got no reason to–"

"Hold up," Boom said, cutting him off. "Before we finish this talk, lemme finish getting set up."

He reached for the electronic device on the table and pressed a button on the side. A small, green light came on. He then lifted the wand and passed it over the items Solomon had removed from his pockets. He then approached the man and waved the wand the full length of his body. He told him to, "Turn around," so he could do the same to his back.

In the meantime, Asha walked to a stereo that was sitting on the floor in the corner of the room. She knelt to turn it on. Suddenly, rap music began to play, loudly. Asha knew Solomon was confused about the music, just as she had been when Boom put her through this same process the first time she met him. Boom was a mean sonofabitch that day, but he was gracious enough to explain that the music was to prevent a law enforcement agency from eavesdropping on them with a high-tech listening device, if they happened to be parked around the corner. That had been her first taste of how careful and diligent this hitman was.

Solomon heard Boom when he told him, "You can turn back around," but he had to strain his ears. He saw that the Jamaican girl, presumably *Brionna*, stood by her man's side now. They were both on the other side of the table.

"You think I'm wearing a wire?" Solomon asked, nearly shouting.

Boom frowned at him and said, "Don't raise your voice. Talk normal. I can hear you, just like you can hear me."

"Okay," Solomon said, not sure if he should feel relieved or alarmed by what was happening. "We good?" he asked. "Can we get down to business?"

Boom nodded. "First I wanna know why you called me. It's a dozen hitters in this city. Some of 'em pretty good. Why you ain't call none of them?"

"I didn't wanna call somebody who was pretty good," Solomon explained. "I only wanted to fuck with the best."

"After what you *think* I did to yo brother, his daddy and yo daughter, you want to do business with me? That don't make no sense."

Asha found it amusing Boom used the word *think* in regard to what they did to the man's daughter. Solomon may not have proof of the two murders, but he was an eyewitness and victim of the daddy-daughter time danger.

"That's water under the bridge," Solomon said. "The last time we talked, I told you I ain't into that revenge shit. That only leads to me looking over my shoulder, waiting for somebody *else* to get revenge. It's hard to make money that way."

Solomon *had* told them that, and it turned out to be true. He didn't even hire anyone to avenge his own brother's death, because it would be bad for business.

"Let's say I believe you," Boom said. "Who is it you want me to meet with?"

"A'ight, bet," Solomon said. He rubbed his hands together, glad they were getting somewhere. "It's more than one person. I don't know if you know, but ever since Mr.

Brown got hisself killed, the streets been warring. Everybody trying to take over the top spot."

Asha appreciated how he referred to Mr. Brown's getting his brain blown out of the back of his head as, *"Got hisself killed."* She had to stop herself from grinning.

"I'm smart enough to know warring ain't gon' get me nowhere near the top," Solomon continued. "I'll just be another crab in the bucket. But if a few of them other niggas wasn't around no more..." He grinned. "They cliques will be too busy trying to pull theyselve together than take over the city. Matter of fact, they'll probably start fighting each other, to see who gon' be the new leader. In the meantime, they'll still be beefing with all these other factions. The only ones smart enough to keep our hands clean and keep expanding our territory is gon' be me and my crew. That's what I need you for."

Boom nodded. So far, everything Solomon said fit into the person Boom believed him to be. Money had always been his only motivation.

"How many people you need me to meet?" Boom asked.

"Five or six," Solomon said. "Five for sure, maybe the other one after I see how things is playing out."

"I'm sure you got names..."

"Yeah, I got names. I got some intel too..."

Solomon rattled off a list of gangstas, some of whom Boom had heard of, others he hadn't. *Slim* and *Pacman* were lieutenants in Mr. Brown's organization. Last Boom heard, Slim was poised to take over where Mr. Brown had left off. Boom had actually planned to go after Slim before he and Asha killed Mr. Brown. But after taking out the head of the organization, there was no need to go back for the tail.

Boom had also heard about Lynx and was surprised he was among the list of soon-to-be casualties. He knew Lynx was an up-and-comer but hadn't heard that he had reached the level of notoriety that would warrant his removal. But Solomon was right about the tendency of thugs to try to fill a power vacuum. In times like this, you could go from being a corner boy to a millionaire in a matter of months, if you played your cards right.

"If I take this job," Boom said, "you don't get no bulk rate. It's 30 a pop, 40 for Slim, and you don't got no stake in whatever money I take off 'em. Anything that fall in my hand, I keep."

"I ain't got no problem with that. I don't want nothing them niggas got – except for them to be gone."

Boom nodded. "Alright. I'll be in touch. Be ready to pay me every time I call. I already told you I need half up front. If I decide to see Slim first, you owe me 20 thou'." He looked down at the belongings Solomon had placed on the table. He hadn't mentioned the stack of bills when Solomon first put it there, but now the stack was of interest.

"I already got you covered," Solomon said. "That's for you," he said, referring to the money. "We done? It's okay if I leave?"

Boom nodded. "Yeah, we good."

No one spoke again, while Solomon retrieved the rest of his belongings and left the house. Boom followed him to the door and locked it behind him. He gathered his wire tap detector and turned off the lights and stereo before meeting his woman in the garage. Asha had already placed the shotgun in the trunk and settled into the passenger seat. They didn't speak to each other until they made it to the freeway.

Boom was the first to ask, "What you think?"

"I think he telling the truth."

"Yeah, me too."

"I'm glad to have all the jobs at once, but we only looking at 140, if we do all six," she calculated.

"Unless we get some paper off all of 'em," Boom countered. "I know all them niggas paid."

"That mean we can't catch 'em in the street. We got a better chance of getting some money out they house."

"Yup." Boom nodded.

"But that mean it's more dangerous," Asha continued. Boom continued to nod.

"Maybe we should just snatch Solomon – hold his ass for ransom. That nigga gotta be worth a few mil'."

Boom looked over at her with a grin. "You sure are wishy washy, when it come to when you wanna keep yo integrity."

"I'm just playing," she said.

"Yeah, you say that now. I bet if I woulda agreed with you, you'd be all for it."

She laughed. "*No, Enzo*. I'm a good girl."

He rolled his eyes. "Now I know you full of shit."

CHAPTER 15

A FEW DAYS later, Asha stepped out of the shower at five pm and went to her spacious closet in search of an outfit that was stylish but not too sexy for a family gathering. That night, her cousin Tristan was celebrating his 30th birthday. His father, Uncle Lucius, was hosting a party that was shaping up to be their biggest family gathering in years. Even Asha's sister had RSVP'd. Asha hadn't seen Gloria since she moved away to an undisclosed location, in hiding after her family was threatened by Mr. Brown's goons.

Asha hadn't spoken to her sister very often in the past six months. She knew Gloria hadn't forgiven her for the role she played in the drama. That was understandable because Asha had yet to forgive herself. Each time she imagined her sister's family on their knees with assault rifles pointed at their faces, it made her feel like she had to throw up. She prayed Gloria would allow her to make amends tonight, and they could salvage their relationship.

In the bedroom, Boom reclined on the king-size mattress, half watching his woman through the open bathroom door, half watching old boxing matches of Iron Mike in his prime.

"You sure you don't wanna come with me?" Asha called from the closet.

He shook his head. "You know I can't be hanging around no house parties."

"It's mostly gon' be outside. My Uncle's firing up the grill."

"That don't make it no better. Matter of fact, being outside makes niggas think they got a clean getaway, if some shit pop off."

"You think somebody in my family would try to hurt you?"

"No, but I'm sure everybody at that party not gon' be one of yo relatives. I got a lot of enemies. They all hoping for the day they catch me slipping."

"Does that mean you can't *never* go to a party?"

"Not right now I can't. If that's the trade I gotta make to stay alive, I'm okay with it."

Asha considered that. "If that's the case, maybe I shouldn't go, either. I know I got some enemies by now..."

"Naw, you'll be alright. Plus you said yo sister might show up. You need to try to make things right with her, if you can. Once we retire and move away from this city, things will be different. We can make some new friends and start living a regular life."

The prospect of that scenario made Asha's heart flutter.

"You want me to bring you a plate from my Uncle's?" she asked.

"Yeah, that'd be nice. Ain't had no good 'cue in a while."

She stepped out of the closet wearing high waisted shorts with an off the shoulder blouse. Boom's dick began to respond to her physique, but he subdued his urges. He loved his woman dearly, but tonight, he wanted to be left alone.

"What you gon' be doing while I'm gone?" she asked.

"Nothing. Same thing I'm doing now."

"Good," she said. "You need a peaceful night." She returned to the bathroom to do her hair. "Is that Tyson you watching?"

"Yup."

"Is he winning?"

"These old videos," Boom replied. "He always win, just like us."

CHAPTER 16

HE WAITED TILL moonrise before he entered the closet and selected his disguise for the night. He didn't lie to his woman often, but if he could get away with doing his jobs solo from here on out, he would. Seeing Asha with a dead dog on top of her had traumatized him. He wouldn't deny her if she had asked to accompany him, but he was okay, if not grateful, that she already had other plans.

Thirty minutes later, he checked himself in the mirror. Tonight, he was not Boom. He was Goldie – a flamboyant baller from Houston with frizzy cornrows, a mouthful of gold teeth, designer glasses, and almost as many moles on his face as Morgan Freeman. The biggest challenge this disguise posed was the natural urge to scratch the moles off his cheeks. They weren't uncomfortable, but he felt them there, as you'd feel a spider's web you'd mistakenly walked into.

He gathered the weaponry he thought he'd need for the job and took off, headed for one of his safehouses on the south side of town. Once there, he swapped his Charger for a GMC Savana. The van was as ugly as it was conspicuous. It wasn't speedy, but with no windows in the back, it was perfect for his mission.

He made a few phone calls when he left the safehouse. His first contact on that side of town either didn't want to get involved or didn't know anything about Pacman's operation. His second contact couldn't point him to the man himself, but he knew the location of one of Pacman's dope houses.

Before heading in that direction, Boom made another call. OG Cali had no stake in the war Solomon had spoken of, and he was always down for a caper. Each time Boom reached out to him, the reward was well worth it.

After explaining his plan, Cali asked him, "How many men you need?"

"I should be good with three."

"No problem."

"And I need to borrow a brick of that white," Boom said.

"Alright. You want that *Medellín* or some shit that's been stepped on?"

"Better make it the Medellín," Boom said. "These niggas might wanna taste it."

"No problem."

"I'm looking like a straight up *mark*," Boom warned him. "Driving a white van. Tell yo niggas not to shoot me when I pull up."

Cali laughed at that. "A'ight, my nigga. I got you."

CHAPTER 17

WHEN BOOM REACHED the corner house that he'd been told was part of Pacman's organization, he spotted two men standing outside. Normally he would circle the property, at least once, to gather more intel, but his van was too noticeable. The men were sure to be wary of him. He didn't want them to start shooting before he had a chance to play his role.

He pulled to a stop directly in front of the house, as if he had every right to be there. He hopped out of the van with both hands exposed.

"*Yo, what it do, nephews*!" he announced. "I'm here to see Pacman. He here? I got a proposition that's gon' make him very happy!"

He walked towards them without a care in the world, his smile showing off his gold grill.

"Say, who the fuck is you?" one of them asked.

"Hey, nigga, hold up," the other one said. He reached into his front pocket and produced a small pistol. He didn't point it at Boom, but the threat was duly noted.

"Yo, it ain't gotta be all that," Boom said. He stopped midway down the walkway and raised his hands. *"I come in peace, Kemosabe!"* He continued to grin foolishly. "Just trying to get in touch with Pacman. Got some business he gon' be interested in. It's gon' benefit y'all too, so ain't no need for no gunplay."

The men gave each other looks before returning their attention to Boom. The one on the left did not put his gun away.

"Nigga, where you from?" the gunman asked.

"H-Town!" Boom said, beaming. "Just rolled in tonight. Niggas call me *Goldie*, and I know you can see why! *You see me over here shining!"*

In addition to his gold teeth, Boom wore two gold chains and a few gold rings that were just as expensive.

"I'm all about my paper," he said, "trying to turn y'all niggas on to a *lick*! Is Pacman here? I ain't saying I don't wanna work with y'all *personally*, but what I'm talking about is *major*! I think it's proper etiquette to run it by the boss man first. I know that's how it is in my neck of the woods. I'm pretty sure it's the same over here in the Meadows."

The men continued to frown, not sure what to make of him.

"Hey, Win!" one of them called into the house.

From inside, Boom heard someone say, "What up?"

"Say, come out here, fool," the other man said. "Some nigga out here talking 'bout he wanna see Pacman."

The man named Win appeared in the doorway a few moments later. He was older than the other two and equally skeptical. He remained safely inside the house, rather than step onto the porch. He looked Boom up and down, his eyes narrowed.

"Who the fuck is you?"

"*Goldie from H-Town*! They call me Goldie 'cause I'm always *shining*. Nigga, you see it. *You see a nigga over here grinding and shining!*"

The man in the doorway chuckled. "This nigga can't be serious."

"Shit, I'm serious as a heart attack!"

"What you wanna see Pacman for?" Win asked, growing frustrated with him.

"I'm trying to do some expanding," Boom explained. "I got my turf in H-Town sewed up. Ain't no more room to grow, unless I start busting some heads. But I ain't trying to move like that. I know y'all doing y'all thang up here, but I bet you ain't never seen no shit like what I'm selling. Got that straight *Hillary Clinton*, fresh off the boat! Y'all put this shit on the street, and it's game over! Ain't nobody gon' be able to fuck with y'all. Tell Pacman that if he looking for something that's gon' change the game around here, Santa Claus has arrived!"

"This nigga 12," the one with the gun guessed.

"Damn near entrapment, if he is," Win said.

"I'm a lot of things," Boom said. "But po-lice ain't one of 'em. I been respectful with you niggas, but that respect shit gotta go both ways. Why don't you call Pacman, if he ain't here, and let me deal with him man-to-man? If he like what I got to show him, he can check my pedigree. It's a *million* niggas down south who'll vouch for me."

"Why don't you show me what you got for him?" Win said, stepping onto the porch. "If I like what I see, I'll gave that nigga a call."

"*Finally, nigga*," Boom said, turning back to his van. "You gon' love this shit. No doubt!"

"Go with 'em," Win instructed the gunman.

Boom had no problem with that. So far, everything was going as he'd expected.

He opened the van on the driver's side and reached to the passenger seat for the brick of cocaine Cali had loaned him. He backed out of the van and saw the man with the gun was right behind him. Boom continued smiling as he walked back to the house.

"*This* what I'm talking about," he said to Win. "Got 20 more in the back! You need to call Pacman and tell him I'ma let these birds fly for the low-low. I'm telling you, shit 'bout to change around here! If y'all get in on the ground floor, you gon' have the best plug in the south, *gua-ran-teed*!"

Win was intrigued now. "Lemme see that," he said, reaching for the dope.

Only a fool would hand it over so easily.

Boom handed it to him.

"Yeah, nigga," he said grinning. "Now you see why a nigga over here shining! *I know y'all niggas see me*!"

"I don't know what y'all got going on in Houston," Win decided, "but you dumb as fuck. Just gon' give me the dope? And you talking about you got 20 more? Even my son know better than that."

Boom's smile slipped for the first time. "Now, I know y'all ain't finna do what I think you finna do. When a cow bring you some milk, you don't disrespect him. You milk that motherfucker."

"Nigga, I am finna milk yo crazy ass," Win said. "And when I'm done milking you, you'll be lucky if we send you back to Houston with yo tail between yo legs. Matter of fact, you'll be lucky if you make it off this block."

Boom shook his head in disappointment. "Fuck y'all niggas. Gimme my shit."

Win's free hand balled into a fist. "Reach over here if you want to. Hey, go see what that nigga got in the van," he told the unarmed man. "If this nigga make one move, pop him," he said to the one with the gun.

"You fucking with the wrong one," Boom said.

"Shut the fuck up," Win spat.

The unarmed man went to the back of the van and pulled the door open. He was greeted by a team of heavily armed, masked men. Cali and his crew were out of the van in an instant.

"Get the fuck back! Back up, nigga!"

Two of them charged the men standing in front of the house, with assault rifles raised and ready to fire. The third hung back and got the straggler in line.

"Get over there, nigga! Move!"

The man armed with the pistol wavered in indecision before realizing they were outmatched and outgunned.

"Nigga, drop that shit, before I bust yo ass!" Cali ordered.

He dropped the gun.

Boom did not look around to watch his associates in action. His eyes remained on Win. When Win's attention returned to his gold teeth, Boom smiled and hit him with Lauren Hill lyrics. Knowing his vocal limitations, he would never sing in public. But Goldie from H-Town was quite the crooner.

"It could all be so simple. But you'd rather make it haaaaard!" He laughed. "Gimme my brick, nigga!" He snatched it from Win's limp hand. "What you know about milking the cow?" he asked as they marched the dealers into

the house. "I'ma show you how to milk a motherfucking cow!..."

CHAPTER 18

TEN MINUTES LATER, they had Pacman's dope house under siege. The workers were on their knees in the living room, staring down the barrels of weapons that were clearly designed for war, yet were plentiful in every American city. Cali's men had run their pockets and taken the drugs they'd planned on selling that night. Boom had already decided what he wanted to do with the dealers, but Cali's crew was playing it by ear. Boom was happy to hear one of them was as bloodthirsty as he was.

"*The nerve*," Boom said, staring the men down. "The nerve of you backwoods ass niggas. I'm tempted to put you all down, *you fucking mutts!*"

"You should," one of Cali's men said. "If you don't, they'll come looking for you. Shaka said never leave an enemy behind, or it will rise again and fly at your throat."

Boom was surprised to hear him quoting Shaka Zulu. It was uncommon for the younger generation to know very much about the African Warrior.

"You got a point," he said. "I tried to turn you on to something major," he told Win, "but you too greedy to get blessed. Y'all deserve some bullets, sure enough, but I ain't gon' kill you. I ain't trying to start off on the wrong foot in this country-ass town. I'ma let y'all live so Pacman can get on y'all ass when he see what you cost him. When yo competition start slanging the best shit this city done ever seen, you gon' think long and hard about what you tried to pull on ol' Goldie. Don't y'all niggas see me shining? You thought this was a game?"

The defeated men stared at him with utter contempt.

"Before we leave," Boom said, "y'all niggas need to get naked and hit the do'. We ain't trying to get shot at on our way outta here."

"Ain't nobody gon' shoot at y'all," Win protested. "You done took our straps."

"Fuck that," Cali said through his ski mask. "I know y'all got some more pistols up in here. Soon as we walk out, you gon' reach for 'em. Y'all better take them clothes off, before Goldie change his mind. My nigga cutting y'all a break, but don't take his kindness for weakness!"

Boom shouldn't have found it so satisfying to see three naked men running down the dark street, but he couldn't deny how good it made him feel.

CHAPTER 19

WHEN IT CAME to dope houses, Boom knew there was one scenario that was guaranteed to draw out the re-up. Waiting for the dealers to run out of drugs was the slow route. A robbery shortened the waiting game. Boom had employed that tactic countless times. It was efficient but not necessarily foolproof. Sometimes a low-level dealer showed up, rather than the top dog he was looking for. And he had taken out so many top dogs with this method, he worried they'd wise to the game.

For tonight's job, he didn't want to wait for a lieutenant to show up, who may or may not lead him to Pacman. He hoped his Goldie act was enough to draw out the boss man. Pacman would want to know all the details about the robbery. He'd want to know about the H-Town connect his people had cost him. He'd want to hear about it personally.

Boom didn't think he had much time before Pacman came through, but there were things he needed to do to prepare. He had to drop off Cali and his goons, pay them for their services, and book it back to his safe house to change out of his outfit and swap the van for the Charger. When he hit the streets again, he was easily recognizable as *Boom*– gold teeth gone, moles gone, cornrows replaced with a black ball cap, and his fake beard in full flair.

He made it back to Pacman's dope house just in time. There was a pearl white Cadillac parked out front. Boom parked down the street, four houses away. He barely had time to kill his headlights before three men exited the house. One was the man they called Win. The other was a face Boom didn't recognize. He didn't recognize the third man either, but he could tell by his size that it was none other than Pacman. Solomon had told him Pacman got his name because he never came across a plate of *anything* he didn't gobble up.

The man Boom saw waddling to the Cadillac was well over four hundred pounds. He watched the car's suspension buckle when the big man climbed inside. When the Cadillac pulled away, Win remained outside for a few moments, looking around, possibly wondering if Goldie would make another appearance. He turned his back on the Charger as Boom drove by, unaware that the demon was on his boss' tail.

He followed the Cadillac for only ten minutes, before it turned into a residential neighborhood. Boom gave them a little more leeway, because the streets were quiet, and unless Pacman was a fool, he should be on high alert. He waited a few beats before turning the last corner, just in time to see Pacman and the man he was traveling with enter a small home, leaving the Cadillac parked out front.

Boom studied the house. It didn't appear to have more than a few bedrooms, one story. Most of the neighbors had porch lights on, but it was after one a.m., and no one was outside at the moment. He turned right on the next street and saw an alley leading behind the target's house. Like most alleyways in this part of town, it wasn't made for driving. He sighed, hoping he wouldn't have to trek through the overgrown area on foot.

On the next street were more houses that were similar to the homes on the first street. No one was throwing a house party on this block either. Boom made a few turns before finding his way back to Pacman's street, heading in the opposite direction this time. He posted up a safe distance away, and saw the Cadillac was parked in the same spot. He watched the house for several minutes before popping open the center console. He frowned, hoping his eyes were deceiving him. They were not. As meticulous as he was, he realized he didn't transfer his high-tech binoculars to this vehicle. Without them, he could not see through the walls of Pacman's house.

But all hope was not lost. Boom was certain he'd brought his favorite sniper rifle, which was equipped with a night vision scope that also provided thermal imaging. He preferred to use the rifle when he was in his SUV, because there was more room to maneuver. But if he had to poke the long barrel out of the Charger's window for a minute to make sure there were only two people inside the house, he was okay with that.

Before he decided to go to the trunk to retrieve the rifle, he watched the house a while longer. There was nothing fun about surveillance, but Boom was a patient man, and he had come to enjoy the alone time with his thoughts. His keen eyes narrowed when the door of the house swung open five minutes later. Boom was happy to see the man

Pacman had arrived with was leaving the residence. He hoped that meant Pacman was left home alone. But there were a couple of things not quite right about the unidentified man.

For one, even from a distance, Boom could see he was agitated. He looked back several times as he exited the house. Whatever he saw inside seemed to distress him. The second thing Boom noticed was the man toted a large bag he didn't have when they first arrived. The man pulled the door closed but didn't appear to lock it. He moved quickly to the Cadillac, stumbling once on legs that were indecisive. He popped the trunk of the Cadillac and tossed the bag inside before hurrying to the driver's side. He didn't peel off, but by the time he passed Boom, he was traveling faster than the 35 miles per hour speed limit in a residential area. He didn't notice Boom's Charger parked in the darkness.

Confused, Boom considered his next move. His target was inside the house, possibly alone with the front door unlocked. But at that moment, he was more interested in the man who had left. He didn't think he could catch up to him, if he handled his business with Pacman first, so he started the car and performed a three-point U-turn on the tight street.

Without the Cadillac, he knew Pacman wasn't going anywhere.

He could wait.

He followed the stranger for fifteen minutes. The drive ended at a seedy motel simply called The Inn. The *Crack* Inn would've been more appropriate. Boom was familiar with the place. At that hour, the only thing moving was crackheads and dealers. The management was okay with all of the shady activities there, as long as everyone paid their rent on time, and the addicts didn't loiter outside too much.

There was a light on in almost all of the occupied rooms. Boom didn't like the chances of a full-frontal assault in a place like this. Kicking the front door would rouse too much suspicion, and the locks on these doors were oftentimes formidable. He decided on another plan of attack as the Cadillac came to a stop in front of room 24. Boom parked on the same row, two cars down, and snatched his pistol from the glove compartment. He exited his vehicle, just as the man he was following removed the bag from the trunk of the Cadillac.

Boom walked to him quickly and shoved the barrel of his Smith & Wesson against his spine.

"Don't say shit," he growled. "And don't look back."

The man went stiff, and he did not speak.

"Which room is yours?" Boom asked him. He looked around and spotted no witnesses, but he couldn't be sure. Crackheads were notorious for peeping through their barely parted curtains.

"Thi, this one," the man said. "Tw, twenty – twenty-four."

"Open it," Boom said, taking the bag from him. "Let the bag go."

The man let go of the bag and walked to the room on jerky, spaghetti legs. Boom remained close, his gun never losing contact with his back. The man was so nervous, his shaky fingers lost control of the keys when he tried to find the one that fit the lock. They fell to the ground.

Boom told him, "That's the first and last mistake you get to make. Pick up those keys and open the motherfucking door. Do one more thing wrong, and it's lights out."

"Don't kill me," the man pleaded as he bent to get the keys. *"Please don't kill me, man."*

"That's gon' be up to you," Boom replied. "Hurry up and open the door."

The man got the door open and stepped inside the motel room. Boom pushed him towards the bed and flipped on the light. Like most of the rooms in this motel, the accommodations were sparse. The main room offered a bed, a dresser and a TV mounted on the wall. There was a nightstand next to the bed, and that was it.

Boom reached back and closed the door.

"Turn around," he ordered.

When the man laid eyes on his abductor, his features stretched into a grimace. Boom had never met him, but his notoriety in the hood was prominent. There was only one bearded goon who moved like this.

By the time you heard that **BOOM!** *it was too late, he'd accomplished his mission.*

"Don't kill me, man," he cried. *"I didn't do nothing! What I do?"*

Boom did not want to spend too much time in the motel, but he couldn't leave until he had the answers he desired.

He started with, "What's yo name?"

"Huh, huh, what?"

Boom raised the gun to his face. "Nigga, stop fucking with me."

"Slimey! They call me Slimey!"

Boom looked him up and down and thought the moniker was fitting.

"What happened over there with Pacman?"

"Huh, what?"

"If you say what one mo' goddamn time…"

"*Nothing!*" Slimey exclaimed. His whole body was trembling. "*He dead, but I didn't do it! I swear I didn't do nothing to him!*"

Boom's ability to discern the truth was almost unparalleled. He knew the man was being honest with him, but it was hard to believe. "What you mean he dead?"

"I don't know what happened to him! He just slumped over. I think that nigga had a heart attack!"

Given the boss' size, that was plausible, but still…

"What's in this bag?" he asked.

"What –" He caught himself. "It's some money and some dope."

"You killed that nigga and took his shit."

"*No, I didn't! I swear*! Me and Pacman is partners. Most of that shit mine! I couldn't leave it there for the laws to find it. I took everything I could and got the hell outta there. All I did was take that shit after he fell over. I didn't kill Pacman! I ain't got no reason to kill him! *That's my nigga!*"

In all his time as a hitman, Boom never had the fortune, or *misfortune*, to not be able to accomplish a mission because the target died on his own.

"Let me tell you something," he said, "I'm finna go over there to check on what you saying. If I see that Pacman got some bullet holes or you done strangled him, I'm coming back for yo ass."

"*I didn't shoot him! You ain't gon' see nothing like that!*"

Boom didn't doubt that was true, because he hadn't heard any gunshots.

"I'm taking this bag with me," he said. "If I go over there, and everything is what you said, I'll bring it back. If it ain't, I'ma do you just like you did him."

"Alright man, fine. You ain't gon' find nothing over there. That nigga died on his own. I swear."

Boom placed the bag on the bed and reached into his back pocket for zip ties. "I gotta put these on you, to make sure you don't try nothing stupid before I get back."

The man stared at the zip ties and decided he was okay with the restraints, if that meant he would keep his life.

"You, you gon' put 'em in the front or the back?"

Boom gave him a hard look that made him pipe down and keep the rest of his questions to himself.

"I'm tying yo hands behind yo back, fuck nigga. What, you think I'm stupid?"

"*No, no sir!*" Slimey turned around and put his hands behind his back. "It, it's cool. Do what you gotta do."

CHAPTER 20

BACK AT PACMAN'S place, Boom found everything as Slimey said it would be. In the kitchen, the big man had fallen out of his chair. He lie on the floor, eyes half open, his face purplish, with foam drooling from his mouth. Boom checked his pulse to make sure, but his eyes were not deceiving him. The fat man was dead. His body showed no signs of trauma.

Boom had encountered plenty of corpses in his time, but this sight was a little unnerving. He would never understand how someone could *eat* themselves to death. Dying from something like a drug overdose was just as dumb. But living a life of gluttony to the point where it became difficult to breathe or even walk and then dying like this was a special kind of self-destruction.

He wondered if Slimey had left more drugs or money behind when he hurried to flee the scene. He decided against searching for it. The bag he took from Slimey was fairly weighty. It didn't feel like half a million dollars, but it felt like enough to make this whole venture worth it. If

Slimey was at the motel waiting for him to untie him and return the bag, he was a fool. If he one day decided to try to find Boom and retrieve his bag, he was an even bigger fool.

On the way home, Boom received the call he'd been waiting for.

When he answered, Asha asked him, "Where you at?"

He told her, "I'm on my way. Had to run a few errands."

"*Had to run a few errands*?"

"We'll talk about it when I get there."

CHAPTER
21

SHE WAS WAITING for him in the kitchen when he entered from the garage. She looked as beautiful as she had the last time he saw her. The only thing missing was her lovely smile.

He asked her, "How was the party?"

"Where were you?"

"I told you, I had to run an errand."

"Not with that beard." She folded her arms under her chest. "You did a job without me."

"Just a little one," he said. "It was light work. Here, I brought you something."

He placed the bag on the counter. If Asha was interested in it, it didn't show.

"Enzo, why would you do that? Do you think that's fair to me?"

"I didn't think you needed to be on *every* job I do. You still have your solo missions."

"Yeah, but at least you know where I am the whole time. Hell, you follow me and don't tell me till afterwards.

What if something had happened to you? I wouldn't have no way to help you, if I don't even know where you at. How you think it make me feel, I'm out at my uncle's having fun, while you putting yo life in danger?"

He moved closer to give her a hug. She pushed him away.

"No, Enzo, that ain't right. I feel like you lied to me. You prolly planned on doing this the whole time, talking about you just gon' stay home and watch some boxing."

Boom had to put aside how cute she looked when she was mad and take her concerns seriously. "I'm sorry, baby. You right. I shouldn't have done that without telling you. I won't do it again."

She continued to frown at him for a few seconds before asking, "Well, what'd you do? You went after somebody on Solomon's list?"

Boom was grateful she'd forgiven him so easily. "Yeah," he said. "I went after Pacman. But that fat fuck died before I got to him."

Her frustration transitioned to confusion.

"Come to the den," he said. "I'll tell you about it, while we count this money..."

Thirty minutes later, Boom went to the kitchen to wash his hands. Back in the den, there were several stacks of bills on the coffee table next to the money counter. Next to the money were a few large bags of narcotics – rocked up cocaine this time. Their haul was a little over 150 thousand. With the crack, they might be looking at 170. Boom returned to the den when he was done washing his hands.

"Bad thing is," he said, "We gon' lose that 30 Solomon was supposed to pay us for taking Pacman out."

Asha sat on the sofa, watching him. "How you figure? That nigga dead, ain't he?"

"Yeah, but I didn't kill him. When I tell 'em Pacman died on his own, we not gon' get paid."

"Tell him you choked that nigga out."

"If I had found him like that on my own, I might try that," Boom said. "But Slimey gon' tell his people the real story. When it get back to Solomon that I lied, it ain't gon' be a good look. That nigga got too much money for me to fuck him over thirty thousand. It ain't worth it. He liable to come up with some mo' people he want killed after we done with this list. I'ma stay in that nigga's pocket for as long as I can."

"I can't believe you hired some *nobody niggas*, when you coulda took me," Asha said, pouting again.

"What nobody niggas?"

"Cali and them. They can't do nothing I can't do. It's bad enough you did the job without me. But then you turn around and get somebody else to help you. That's some shady shit, Enzo."

"Damn, woman. Are you gon' shut up about this? I done already apologized."

Her lips curved into a sneer. "*Shut up*? Why don't you make me shut up?"

Boom could've walked away, but this time he took her up on the offer. He walked to her, positioned himself between her legs and pulled his dick out in one smooth motion.

"I don't know what you think–"

He grabbed the back of her head with one hand and his dick with the other. He cut her off by shoving his meat in her mouth. Asha grunted her disapproval, but she didn't do anything drastic like bite.

"I told you to shut up," he said.

She hummed something around his dick that may have been, "*You can't make me.*"

And then she started sucking. There was something forbiddingly erotic about her sucking his dick while staring up at him with angry eyes. It was something Boom had never experienced. He wasn't prepared for how good it felt.

He came in a matter of minutes.

Asha may have been upset with him, but she didn't let one drop spill.

PART THREE
LOOSE LIPS

CHAPTER
22

THE NEXT MORNING, Boom called Solomon to set up a meeting. The hood millionaire said he'd be free at two p.m. Having already vetted him, Boom directed him to a soul food restaurant, rather than send him back to his safe house. He arrived at the location twenty minutes before the scheduled meeting time. Boom knew the owner of the restaurant and felt safe there, but he always had the need to watch his clients' arrival before they knew he was watching them.

Solomon pulled into the parking lot right on time, driving a new Lexus. He was alone, as Boom had instructed. The drug lord parked amongst the other diners and called Boom on one of his burner phones. Rather than answer, Boom approached the Lexus on the passenger side. Solomon unlocked the door when he noticed him standing there.

"Man, you like a thief in the night," Solomon commented when Boom sat next to him. "I didn't see you coming."

Boom didn't respond to that. Instead he said, "Did you hear about Pacman?"

"Yeah," Solomon said grinning. "The streets is already talking."

"I was ready to do the job," Boom informed him. "I was right outside his house when he died."

"Oh, I thought you got 'em and set it up to make it look like a heart attack."

Boom shook his head, wondering if he should've taken Asha's advice and took credit for the big man's death.

"Oh, well. Good riddance," Solomon said. "I can't believe that nigga went out like that. I will never understand how a motherfucker can fuck around and *eat* hisself to death."

"Yeah, I was thinking the same."

"You know something," Solomon said, "you a straight shooter. I like that about you. You coulda told me you was the reason Pacman took his last breath, but you didn't. I like a nigga that keep it one hundred."

Boom nodded.

"Well, if you worried about not getting that payment," Solomon continued, "I got something to make it up to you."

That got Boom's attention.

"Pacman had a running buddy named *Slimey*," Solomon reported. "It ain't even been 24 hours since Pacman died, and Slimey already making moves to pick up where he left off. He ain't a big problem *yet*, but I figure I might as well knock him off before he get too big for his britches. You ever heard of Slimey – know anything about him?"

Boom was glad he'd let the man live last night. Solomon was offering to pay him to do something he almost did for free.

"Yeah, I think I heard of him," he replied.

"You can take care of that for the same thirty you was gon' get for Pacman?"

"Yep. That's light work. Pretty sure I can get it done tonight. I'll give you a call when I'm done."

CHAPTER 23

THAT NIGHT, BOOM was on his second stakeout in as many days. His partner in crime was with him. Asha would've had a conniption if he tried to leave her behind, but he actually preferred to have her with him this time.

At 11pm, they sat in the parking lot of an auto parts store across the street from The Inn. The parts store was closed for business. Asha was in the driver's seat of a black SUV. Boom watched the scene before them from the backseat. They'd already entered and then left The Inn, without spotting the Cadillac Slimey was driving the night before. There was a chance he was in a different car, but Boom banked on him keeping the pearl-colored Cadillac. He also banked on Slimey not being wary of a woman driving an SUV.

"You sure he coming back here?" Asha asked.

They'd only been on surveillance for forty minutes. Boom knew she hadn't mastered the art of patience as well as he had.

"No, I'm not sure," he acknowledged. "But this is the last place I seen him, so he might have some ties here."

"I wouldn't come back – not after somebody tied me up and jacked me."

"Yeah," Boom said, his eyes on the only entrance and exit to the motel. "I'm sure you wouldn't."

"But you think his thinking is different."

Boom sighed. He knew she wouldn't let it go until he fully explained his thought process. Any other time, he'd find this irritating. But for a partner like Asha, it was acceptable.

"I think he's thinking he's okay," he explained. "When I saw him last night, I told him I was after Pacman. Since I let him live, he knows I wasn't lying about that. With Pacman out of the picture, I'm sure Slimey thinks he's in the clear. If so, he may think it's okay to keep working his same spots."

After a couple of beats, Asha said, "If not? What's your Plan B?"

"I know where one of Pacman's dope houses is," Boom replied. "We can stake out that place, if he don't show up here."

"What if he don't show up there?"

"What if I leave yo ass at home next time? I ain't got no problem watching houses till morning, but it seems like you do."

She looked back and gave him a look. "You ain't gotta be so damn rude."

"You ain't gotta be questioning me all the time. When have you known me to be wrong?"

Asha was about to point out several occasions.

But Boom said, "And while you over here giving me funny looks, you missing the *one thing* you supposed to be looking for. If you *was* looking, you'd see that I was right – as always."

Asha turned back and saw the taillights of a white Cadillac entering the motel.

"That's him?"

"Yeah. Give him a few seconds before you go in there."

She started the car and waited.

"You can't bring yourself to tell me I was right," Boom noticed.

"Maybe this time," she said and put the truck in gear. "But you ain't *always* right."

Boom rolled his eyes. "I swear, if you was a nigga, I woulda decked you in the back of the head by now."

She laughed at that. "Well, thank God for this good pussy!"

Inside the motel, Boom instructed her to hang back, until they saw which room Slimey was headed for. When he realized it was room 24, he readied his weapon and told Asha to move closer. He planned to intercept Slimey like he had last night, force him into the room and handle his business there. But Slimey didn't exit his vehicle this time. Instead, the door of room 24 opened, and someone stepped out.

"Hold up," Boom said to Asha. "Hold what you got…"

They watched as the unknown man approached the Cadillac. Slimey rolled down the window, and they conducted a brief transaction. The man gave Slimey cash in exchange for a Walmart bag. The man returned to the room, and Slimey put the Cadillac in reverse. Both Asha and Boom had seen this scenario many times.

"Slimey the re-up now?" Asha asked.

"Look like it," Boom said.

"I thought he was working this room last night."

"He was."

"He already got somebody working for him?"

"Solomon said he was taking over where Pacman left off."

"Damn, that fast?"

"I guess so."

"These niggas don't even wait for a nigga to get buried, before they move on without him."

"The streets is heartless," Boom confirmed. "Slimey prolly already fucking Pacman's bitch."

They followed him out of the motel and to several more motels. Asha thought she was driving as well as her man would, but Boom was the ultimate backseat driver.

"Hey, get off his ass," he complained.

"Let that nigga breathe."

"You gotta put some cars between y'all."

"You can't turn right after that nigga."

"Damn, you want this nigga to make us?"

Fed up, Asha finally said, "*Fuck, Enzo. You wanna drive?*"

"No, I want you to do it right," he spat.

"I'm doing it just like you told me."

"Well, do it like I'm telling you now."

When they entered a residential neighborhood, she hoped their surveillance had come to an end, but Boom told her, "This is the house I started at yesterday. You finna see that nigga Win I told you about."

Asha parked a safe distance away and killed the lights. The transaction at this location was no different than the others.

"That nigga must have a grip on him by now," Asha surmised. "I think we should take him in the car, get this shit over with."

Boom gave that some thought. "You don't wanna see if he gon' do some more pickups?"

"We ain't gotta be greedy. He by hisself. No telling who gon' be at wherever he finally stop."

Boom liked the way she was thinking but asked, "If you was gon' play it like that, how would you do it?"

"Shit, pull up next to him and let it fly. Hop out and get the money."

"Fuck it," Boom decided. "But if you get him on a main street, you gotta watch out for traffic light cameras. I don't wanna have to get rid of this truck."

"I can get him in the neighborhood."

"You sure about that?"

"You gon' let me try?"

By then Slimey was on the move again, and so were they.

Boom wasn't completely sold on the plan, but he told her "Alright. Go 'head."

When they approached the next intersection, Asha moved in closer than she had all night. She stopped directly behind the mark and made the same turn after the stop sign.

"He know you on him now," Boom said.

"That's alright," she said, focused on her driving. "I'm 'bout to end this."

Asha wanted to intercept on the next street, but there were too many cars parked alongside the curb. They were reduced to one lane. To make matters worse, the Cadillac began to accelerate.

"*Fuck*," she breathed.

Boom didn't bother with an I told you so, because it wasn't her plan at that point. They were in it together.

"Want me to chase him?" she asked.

"Got no choice," Boom said. "Stay on his ass."

She jammed her foot on the accelerator as the Cadillac did the same. Slimey sped through the next intersection, ignoring the stop sign. Asha had no choice but to follow suit.

"Shit."

She really wished Boom was driving now, not just to cut down on the complaints, but he had more experience with high-speed chases. But he was content and focused as he stared at the target through the front windshield.

"It's a T-bone coming up," he said knowingly. "He gon' have to slow down to make that turn. When he do, ram the shit outta his ass."

Asha's grip on the steering wheel was tight, her breathing shallow. Her thoughts raced as fast as the two cars. This was the exact opposite of a typical Boom mission. His targets never saw him coming until it was too late. Oftentimes, he took his targets down from a distance, and they never saw him at all. She tried to do it differently this time, and she had failed. The guilt of letting her man down somehow overrode her adrenaline rush.

"I'm sorry," she said.

"Ain't shit to be sorry about," he said, his eyes glued to the Cadillac. "The turn is coming. Be ready."

She shook off her emotions and focused on the job at hand. She kept her foot on the accelerator as they neared the T-bone, planning to hit the Cadillac so hard all four wheels left the pavement as it rolled into the vacant lot ahead of them. But as luck would have it, she didn't have to do a thing.

Apparently Slimey didn't know the neighborhood as well as Boom did. By the time he realized he could not go straight on the street ahead of them, it was too late. He slammed the brakes, and the Cadillac's tires screeched before colliding with the curb, hard enough to break the axle and deploy the airbags. The car jumped the curb and made it almost all the way onto the field before coming to a stop.

Asha slammed on her brakes and came to a stop right behind it. She thought the collision was incapacitating and was surprised to see the Cadillac's door fly open and a man stumble out. She thought Slimey had plenty of time to arm himself as they pursued him. If so, he must have lost his piece when he wrecked. She reached for her own weapon, but Boom was way ahead of her. She didn't notice him get out of the car, but her dark man was suddenly bathed in her headlights. He rushed the target and kicked Slimey's legs out from under him, before the man had a chance to take off.

Boom took aim when the man rolled to his back. He almost pulled the trigger when they locked eyes, but Slimey said something that stopped him cold.

"Wait, Boom! Don't shoot! Don't shoot me! I know Solomon sent you! We can make a deal!"

Boom was rarely stunned by something a marked man told him, but this time he removed his finger from the trigger guard.

"Nigga, what you say?"

Slimey's breathing was erratic, his eyes large. His nose was bloodied by the force of the Cadillac's airbag.

"Please," he said. *"You said you wasn't gon' kill me! You said you was after Pacman!"*

"Why you think Solomon had something to do with this?" Boom wanted to know, his gun trained on his face.

"That's what they saying!" Slimey squealed. "They say Solomon trying to take out the competition!"

"Who? Who said that?"

"I don't know, man. People. The streets."

"If you wanna live, you better give me a name."

"My nigga Win told me! He said Solomon trying to take over the city."

"Win told you Solomon hired *me?*"

"No! He didn't know who he hired, but I knew it was you when you came for Pacman last night. You said you was gon' let me live if I didn't have nothing to do with him dying. If Solomon sent you back for me, we can work something out!"

Boom's expression was as menacing as ever. "Something like what?"

"I can pay you whatever Solomon paid you to kill me, and then I can pay you double to go after him. I got–"

Boom shut him up with two to the head.

BLAK!-BLAK!

He casually walked away from the body, as if he'd done nothing but take out the trash. Before returning to Asha, he checked the Cadillac. He retrieved a large Gucci bag and marched back to his SUV. The anger in his eyes was enough to make Asha cringe, though she knew it wasn't directed at her. He got into the passenger seat brooding. Asha put the car in gear and drove away.

"What he say?" she asked. "I heard him say something about Solomon."

"He say he know Solomon sent somebody to kill him," Boom said, without looking her way.

Asha was confused. Her blood ran cold. "What that mean, Solomon running his mouth?"

"No, I don't think he that stupid. But if these niggas know I'm coming for 'em, that changes everything." He dug his phone from his pocket.

"What you gon' do?" Asha asked.

"I'ma call Solomon." He looked for the unsaved number in his recent calls. "We finna get to the bottom of this."

CHAPTER 24

SOLOMON AGREED TO meet them at the same restaurant they met at earlier that day. Boom got there first. He was behind the wheel of the SUV now, with Asha on the passenger side. He didn't speak much while they waited for the client, but he did say he might have to cut Solomon off.

"If this nigga out there talking my business, we done working for him. I'd hate to turn his money down, but I can't fuck with nobody that's unprofessional."

Asha understood how he felt, on both accounts. They'd only done a couple of jobs for Solomon, but in the past few days they'd gotten closer to acquiring their nest egg than they had in the past two months. She wondered if it might not be time to transition to strictly robbing people. She knew Boom was against that, so she didn't bring it up at the moment. He had enough on his mind.

When Solomon pulled into the parking lot, Boom remained in his car. Solomon parked next to them and came to meet them. He smiled as Boom rolled his window down.

His smile didn't falter when he saw that neither occupant of the SUV were smiling back.

"You got news for me already?" he asked. "I know you said you'd check on Slimey tonight, but I didn't think it'd be that quick."

"I took care of it," Boom told him.

"That's what's up," Solomon said. "Please tell me Slim is next. After him, I think we'll be done with what's left of Mr. Brown's lieutenants."

"I can pay Slim a visit," Boom said. "But first I need to talk to you about something. Slimey said some shit that's got me tripping."

"What that nigga say? What's wrong?"

"He said he knew you hired somebody to come after him," Boom reported. "He said you taking out the leaders of other crews, so you can take over. He called you out by name."

The news didn't seem to bother Solomon as Boom thought it should.

The drug lord said, "Word?"

"Yeah," Boom replied. "And you see why that's a problem, don't you? You been running your mouth about our business?"

"Hell naw. I ain't said shit to nobody."

"Well, how that nigga know you was gunning for him?"

"He prolly just guessing it was me," Solomon surmised. "One of my niggas got into it with him a few weeks ago, but I told him to let that shit be. Slimey prolly think I still had some ill will against him. I do, but he don't know nothing for sure."

"That nigga sounded sure to me," Boom said. "You sure you ain't told *nobody* about your plans?"

"My nigga, I don't fuck around like that. I ain't even got no partner in my organization. I got some lieutenants, but ain't none of 'em my right-hand man. I don't tell them niggas shit about my long-term goals. I tell 'em enough for them to play they part and get paid. This shit with Slimey gotta be a coincidence. That nigga don't know nothing about what me and you got going on."

Boom was usually the one to notice something awry when he was meeting with a client, like a pair of unknown headlights encroaching on their space. He may have been distracted by Solomon, who obstructed his field of view. Asha didn't mention it immediately because she didn't want to interrupt their important meeting with what may have been a false alarm. Her fatal mistake was not speaking up until she heard a car door open.

"Hey," she said to Solomon, "who is that?"

The kingpin half turned and was greeted by a volley of gunshots.

BLAT!BLAT!BLAT!BLAT!

Asha screamed.

Solomon fell out of view.

The gunman, who was little more than a silhouette in the unknown car's headlights, ran to their SUV and continued shooting.

BLAT!BLAT! – BLAT!BLAT!BLAT!

Boom reacted the only way he could. He threw his body over the only thing he truly loved. His strong arms tried to push Asha down, but there was nowhere to go. They were sitting ducks.

Asha continued to scream. *"Enzo!"*

In the aftermath of the shooting, which was over as quickly as it had started, the ringing in Asha's ears rivaled the thunderous pounding of her heart. She still heard the echoes of the gunshots. She did not hear the triggerman speed away. Gradually she heard her man's ragged breathing. She felt pressure. Dead weight. She felt wetness. She didn't know if the blood was hers.

"Enzo, baby. Are you okay? Enzo...!"

Tears streamed down her face as she struggled to free her arms so she could find his face. She needed to see his face. She needed to know if he was alright.

Freeing herself from his sheer bulk was almost impossible. She felt as if she was trapped beneath a dozen sandbags. She didn't want to push him – didn't want to hurt him more than he already was – didn't want to believe her man of steel was really made of flesh and bones that could be destroyed by bullets.

"Enzo, please baby, get up. Baby, please..."

He didn't respond, but his breathing, ragged though it was, let her know that all hope was not lost. He needed help, and time was of the essence. She was the only person in a position to save him. She could let no obstacle hold her back, especially not the weight of Boom's body, which he'd sacrificed in what may have been his final act of love for her.

As forcefully and delicately as possible, she first pushed her door open and then managed to slip from beneath his body. Once out of the car, she was able to see him more clearly. Boom's eyes were half closed, staring at her but not really seeing her. His shirt was soaked with blood, but she couldn't see the wounds. The lack of blood on his face was the only bright spot in this horror show. She knew that he hadn't been shot in the head.

"It's gon' be alright baby. I'ma get you some help."

Getting him to the passenger side was ten times more daunting than prying herself from beneath him, but a part of Boom was alert enough to know that she was trying to save him. He managed to move his legs, while she pulled his upper body. When she got him in the seat, his head rolled on his strong neck as if he was drunk. Asha frantically reached over and fastened his seatbelt, not so much for safety, but because it may be the only thing to stop him from sliding out of the seat.

She slammed the door closed and ran to the driver's side. She had to step over Solomon's body. Whether the millionaire might also survive the attack was never up for debate. He'd been hit at least once in the head. Asha nearly slipped on his brain matter.

She hopped in the truck and threw it in gear. Boom's eyes rolled her way, and he was able to put a sentence together.

"Baby, I'm hit bad."

Asha's face folded in on itself. "Baby, I know," she said. She wiped the tears and snot from her face with her freehand and sped out of the parking lot. "It's gon' be okay," she said, praying she wasn't telling him a lie. *"I'ma, I'ma get you some help, baby. It's gon' be okay..."*

CHAPTER 25

ASHA WISHED THEY were in the Charger. Their Suburban couldn't eat up the freeway quickly enough. Typically, she would never drive this fast, especially after completing a job, but Boom needed urgent care.

She knew he never wanted to find himself a patient in a hospital, but she had no alternative. Boom worried that if he ever did get injured badly enough to require hospitalization, whoever had inflicted the damage would come there to finish him off. That was highly plausible. But Asha would never let that happen. She'd remain by his side 24/7. She'd hire additional security if necessary.

Boom's second concern with hospitals was that the police would be summoned to investigate his injuries, and he'd end up getting arrested for one of his many, many sins. That was also a valid concern, and it was something Asha knew she could do nothing to prevent.

She stroked his leg as she headed downtown, only losing contact with him to wipe her tears, which she was trying her best to get under control.

"Baby, I got you," she told him. *"Say something, Enzo. You gotta stay up. Talk to me, baby, please."*

He hadn't spoken to her since she moved him to the passenger seat. She didn't know if remaining awake and alert was necessary for his survival, but she knew sleep was akin to death. If he didn't fight now, he might not be able to fight when the cold hand of death gripped his and tried to pull him away from the light.

"Baby, talk to me. Please, baby. Say something..."

When he did speak, Asha had been straining her ears for so long, she thought she imagined it. The window on her door was down at the time of the shooting. It had been shattered, inside the door frame. The wind blowing past the SUV made it difficult to hear.

"Wh, what?" She was traveling so fast, it was dangerous to take her eyes off the road, even for a second, but she looked over at him to see if his lips had actually moved. "Baby, you said something? Baby..."

This time she saw his lips move as well as heard him speak. His voice was faint, but she understood what he was telling her. Rather than relief that he was coherent, she frowned at his message.

"Call Doc."

"I'm taking you to the doctor," she said. "I'm on my way to the–"

"No." He shook his head weakly. *"No hospital. Call Doc,"* he repeated.

Despite watching his lips form the words, Asha couldn't believe she'd heard him right.

"What? Call – *Baby no.* I'm not calling that man. I'm taking you to the hospital. You need–"

"Cuh – call him."

She could see it was taking everything he had to get the words out. She didn't want to cause him any more distress than he was already experiencing, but what he was asking her to do was ludicrous.

"*Baby, he's a **vet***! You need to go to the hospital! You need surgery. Enzo, I love you, but I can't do that. I promise I won't let nothing happen to you at the hospital. I promise, baby. *You gotta trust me.*"

Boom struggled to take a few breaths. Asha knew he was trying to repeat his instructions, but he couldn't get the words out.

"*Fuck!*"

She jerked the steering wheel to the right, crossing three lanes in order to take the next exit on the freeway. When she made it to the service road, she pulled over and put the car in park.

"*Enzo. Enzo...!*"

He didn't respond, but he was still breathing. In the darkness, she saw that more blood was soaking his tee shirt.

"*Dammit!*"

She reached and patted his left pocket. She felt the bulge of his phone. She retrieved it and accessed his contacts. Sure enough, only one was saved as, "Doc." She made the call and then got moving again. At the next intersection, she made a U-turn under the underpass. By then, the call had connected to the SUV's Bluetooth. A voice she recognized answered after a few rings.

"Hello."

Asha had to get her thoughts and breathing under control before she could respond.

"Hey, uh, it's, this is Brionna. I came to see you a few weeks ago, got bit by a dog..."

After a pause, the vet said, "Okay. What's wrong? Why are you calling me?"

Asha didn't know if he was always this rude or if he was playing it off while his wife sat up in bed watching him. Either way, her blood began to boil.

"I'm on my way to your office," she said. "Boom's hurt. He told me to call you."

Another pause.

"Put him on the phone."

"He can't talk right now. He told me to call you."

"Why can't he talk right now?"

"I just told you, *he's hurt.*"

"You just told me he said to call me. How could he tell you to call me, if he can't talk?"

"Listen, man. I'm in the car with him. He sitting right next to me. He can't talk, but he told me to call you before he passed out."

She listened to him breathing for a few seconds.

"What's wrong with him?" he asked at length.

Asha's nostrils flared. "*He got shot*," she growled. "Do you live far away from your office? I need you to be there when I get there. I'm about fifteen minutes away."

"Where did he get shot?"

"*I don't know*! Somewhere in the side or the back. I think he got hit more than once."

"If he's in that bad a shape, you need to take him to the hospital."

"He told me—"

"I know Boom doesn't want to go to the hospital," the man said. "But he knows there are limitations to what I can do."

"You do surgeries on horses and cows and shit," Asha spat back. "If you can do that, you can do surgery on him!"

"I don't do *trauma surgeries*. I'm not a *trauma surgeon*!" he replied with as much attitude.

"*You can try*! I'll be there in *ten minutes*. You better fucking be there! If Boom dies in your parking lot, I'ma burn yo shit to the ground!"

"Don't you threaten me!"

"I'm sorry – I..." She forced herself to tone it down. "I'm sorry. I, I just... Listen, all I'm asking you to do is try to help." She had gotten her tears subdued, but now they flowed anew. "If you try, and he die anyway, that's one thing. But if he die 'cause you wouldn't even show up, I'ma go crazy. Boom know how bad he hurt. But he still told me to call you. That mean he trust you. I'm on my way over there. Please, sir. Please come..."

The next pause was the longest yet. The freeway blurred, while Asha waited for him to respond.

"Alright," the vet finally said. "I'll be there." He disconnected.

CHAPTER 26

WHEN SHE ARRIVED at the animal hospital, the vet was ready to change his mind before even examining the patient. He sat in his Mercedes in front of the main building. His eyes grew large when Asha pulled up next to him, and he saw the blood and bullet holes in the driver's door. He left his vehicle and approached the SUV.

"Holy shit..."

When he looked up at Asha's grief-stricken face, all the color drained from his.

"This is his blood?"

Asha shook her head numbly. She knew that in addition to the blood on the side of the car, he must have seen bits of Solomon's brain too.

"Somebody else was standing there," she said. "Boom was in the car when he got hit."

The vet moved to the passenger side. Asha rolled the window down, so he could peer into it. Boom was unresponsive, slumped in his seat. His dark shirt was drenched, his face dotted with sweat. Asha hadn't noticed, but there was blood trickling from his mouth now.

"*Fuck*," the vet breathed.

He could see that Boom was still breathing, but he checked for a pulse on his neck. He shook his head grimly. He looked up at Asha, with an expression she would describe as disappointment, before backing away.

"You brought him here to die," he decided.

"Don't say that. You said you'd try to help."

"I will, but I want you to know what you did. You should've bit the bullet and took him to the hospital." He shook his head again and sighed. "Follow me around back."

At that moment, Asha knew she would kill this man. She had told him she'd accept the outcome of his efforts, as long as he tried to help, but she no longer believed she could do that. Doc's callousness in this dire situation hardened her heart and made her blood run cold. She watched him return to his car and drive to the side of the building. She put her truck in gear and followed him.

Doc opened the gate, as he'd done the last time they were there, and continued driving. Rather than stop at the rear of the hospital, he led her to one of the adjacent buildings. He parked and exited his vehicle again.

Before heading inside, he told Asha, "I'm gonna get a table for him. It won't roll very well on this gravel, so I'll need your help getting him inside."

Asha was confused about what he was fetching until he returned with a mobile lift table. She knew a stretcher was better suited for the job, which was another reminder that this man did not have the proper equipment to care for humans. She cursed herself for not overriding Boom's decision to bring him here. Contrary to his boast, he was not always right. This mistake could cost them everything.

Doc rolled the table across the gravel parking lot and told Asha to open Boom's door. When she did, he slumped in that direction. She had to hold him up, while the vet got the table as close as he could.

"I need your help getting him on here," he said. He applied the brakes on the table and said, "I'll get his upper body. You get his legs."

Asha nodded tensely. "Okay."

"Unfasten his seatbelt."

She did so and got into position, her eyes filled with dread.

Doc reached into the car and worked to get his arms under Boom's. He strained to lift him and then said, "Dammit. I don't think I can do this by myself."

"Want me to—"

"No, no. You stay ready to get his legs. I don't want to move him too much. We could cause more trauma, if we let his legs drag on the ground. I just..."

He tried again, lifting so hard his face turned red, and veins bulged on his forehead. Using all his might, he was able to move the wounded warrior.

"Okay. *Hurry! Grab his legs!*"

Asha hurried to do her part. She knew the doctor had the bulk of Boom's weight, but lifting his legs high enough to get his backside on the table was no easy task. They were both panting by the time they got him in position. The vet wiped the sweat from his brow, subconsciously leaving a smear of blood on his face.

When Asha moved to close the car door, the amount of blood in the seat made her heart squeeze uncomfortably. Doc saw it too.

"He's gonna need some blood," he said. "A lot of it – another thing he could get at the hospital, but not here."

Asha swallowed hard. "So, what do we–"

"Just help me get him inside for now. We'll deal with that later."

CHAPTER 27

ONCE INSIDE THE spacious room, Asha saw that it was equipped for examinations of all sorts of animals, but not necessarily operations. They wheeled the lift table to the center, where the light was the brightest. The vet went to wash his hands and put gloves on before returning to his patient, who was unresponsive but still breathing. Doc used scissors to cut Boom's clothing off – all of it. It was then that Asha saw her man's injuries. She only saw one hole at first, on his upper abdomen, but when Doc rolled him to his side, they saw another bullet hole on his back. Both were seeping blood. The vet's first job was to try to stop the bleeding.

The man worked meticulously and professionally, but he didn't miss an opportunity to remind Asha that this was beyond his scope of expertise.

"He needs an operating room."

"You operate in here, don't you?" she asked looking around. "You do horse surgeries. Ain't this where you do it?"

"Yes, but I don't operate alone. I have assistants and an anesthesiologist to help me. I can't do something like this alone."

Asha was nearly frantic. "I can help you. What you need me to do?" She couldn't fault the vet for the look he gave her. "Just, do what you can," she pleaded.

He frowned and said, "I gotta find the bullets. It doesn't look like either one of them went through and through. They're still in him somewhere..."

"Okay, you..."

"I need X-rays."

Asha's heart shuddered. "Okay, where–"

"Over there," Doc said. He nodded towards an adjacent room, while applying pressure to both of Boom's wounds. "That's my X-ray room."

Asha looked in that direction and felt, for the first time, that this man might actually be able to pull this off.

"I need some tape to hold this gauze down," he told her.

Asha looked around wildly.

"Over there," he said, nodding towards the sink. "Look in the top drawer on the left."

Asha ran to the sink and found what he was looking for. She started a strip and reached to hand it to him.

"No, you do it," the vet said. "I'll lift him up. It needs to go all the way around, as tight as you can get it. I'll keep pressure on these, while you wrap."

Asha's wrapping skills were shoddy at best, but the vet didn't complain when she was done.

"Alright, I'll be back," he said. He disengaged the brakes and wheeled the table into the X-ray room.

Asha waited nervously while he took the internal images.

When he was done, he approached her and said, "It'll take a few minutes for me to look at these. Regardless of what I see, he's gonna need some blood, if he's got any chance of making it."

Asha's continued to stare at him. She had no idea what he wanted her to do about that.

"Boom once told me he had someone who could get his blood type," Doc revealed. "You need to go get it, and you need to hurry."

Asha shook her head. "Wha, he, he never said anything to me about it. I don't, I don't know where he was talking about."

"You'd better figure it out – *fast*. Where's his phone? If he had my number in there, maybe he has the number for whoever is supposed to give him the blood."

Asha didn't think it would be that simple, but she ran out of the building. She'd left Boom's phone in the SUV. She found the bloody device and had to wipe it on her shirt before it recognized her finger taps. She checked the contacts and only found a few numbers that were saved with an actual name or word. One of the contacts was simply labeled "Blood."

Tears filled her eyes as she marveled at her man's resourcefulness. Not for the first time, she realized Boom was always ten steps ahead of everything, even his impending doom.

She called the number.

A male voice answered with a guarded, "Hello."

"Hey," Asha said, suddenly unsure of herself. "Blood" could be anyone. This could simply be a member of the

Blood gang, for all she knew. "Um, Boom told me to call you," she said.

After a few seconds of silence, the man said, "Who's this?"

"That's not important."

"What you mean *that's not important*? Let me talk to Boom."

"He can't talk right now. He's hurt."

"What he tell you to call me for?"

Asha decided to go all in. "He said you could get his blood type. He needs some blood. It's an emergency."

After another pause, the man said, "I need to see Boom. If he can't talk, take a picture of him and send it to me."

"I can't do that," Asha said, knowing Boom would never allow his picture to be floating around.

"Then call me back with a video call, and let me see him."

"I can't do that, either. You might take a screenshot."

"Well, how I know you're calling for Boom?"

"How do you think I got this number? What random person would be calling asking for Boom's blood?"

"I don't know, maybe somebody trying to get me fired."

"Listen, once you see me, you'll know I'm not bullshitting. If you look me in the eyes and still don't trust me, you can gone on about your business." That was the ultimate bluff. If this man showed up with Boom's blood, she'd kill him twice before she'd let him drive away with it.

The man on the other end considered that and then asked, "How many units he need?"

Asha had no idea. She ran back to the X-ray room. Doc was sitting behind a counter now, accessing the images on a laptop.

"He wants to know how many units we need," she told him.

The vet pursed his lips and said, "At least four."

Asha relayed the information to the man on the phone.

He told her, "Meet me in the medical district. Call me when you get there."

Asha couldn't believe that had worked out. Boom had *a guy* for everything!

"Okay," she said and disconnected.

She stepped into the X-ray room and peered over the vet's shoulder. None of the images made sense to her.

Rather than explain them, the vet said, "You know this surgery is gonna cost an arm and a leg."

"That's fine," she said. "I got the money."

Without looking away from his screen, Doc said, "Let's see it."

Asha blew a fuse. *"I told you I'd pay you! This man over here dying, and you asking about some fucking money! Can you worry about saving his life first?"*

The vet remained calm and emotionless. "No, what I'm worried about is you not paying me if I *don't* save him. If you want me to operate, you have to pay up front. And I needed that blood *thirty minutes ago*, so standing here arguing with me isn't a good idea."

Asha almost slapped the shit out of him.

"I don't give a damn if you don't like what I'm saying," the vet said. He didn't have the decency to look her in the eyes. "If you shoot me," he continued, "Boom's definitely gonna die." He turned and faced her then. "If you don't want to pay me, we can wheel this table back to your car, and I'll help you load him up. Otherwise, you need to go get my money, and you need to go get that blood."

Asha's whole body was on fire. She snarled at him before turning and hurrying back to the SUV. She returned with the Gucci bag Boom had taken from Slimey. Back in the X-ray room, she reached into the bag and grabbed a handful of bills. She threw the money at the vet's feet, without knowing how much it was. She threw two more handfuls at him.

Doc was unbothered by her tantrum. He said, "If you think I'm picking that up, you're out of your fucking mind. This is a place of business. I'm a professional, and you will treat me as such. The longer you take to pick up that money and bring me that blood, the less chance Boom has to survive."

Asha screamed in frustration as she dropped to her knees and gathered the money. She slammed it on the counter next to his laptop.

"Alright," the vet said. "Now go get the blood."

She turned and stormed out of the building.

Oh yes, she was definitely going to kill this man. Doc would die if Boom survived. He'd die a lot sooner if Boom didn't make it. Asha prayed his healing hands would work a miracle, but that would only delay the inevitable.

The vet's days were surely numbered.

CHAPTER 28

IT TOOK ASHA 42 agonizing minutes to make it back to Overbrook Meadows. She didn't want to push it too far over the speed limit, because her truck looked like an active crime scene. If she got pulled over or – *God forbid* – arrested, Boom was a goner. She was the only link between the vet and the blood Boom so dreadfully needed.

When she reached the city limits, she headed to the hospital district and called the blood contact.

"What's up?" he answered. "You made it?"

"I'm close. Where you want me to head?"

"You know where Jackson Memorial is?"

"Yeah."

"There's a QuikTrip around the corner, on Rosedale."

"I can't go to a gas station. My car too messed up. I can meet you on one of the side streets."

"Oh. Okay. When you get to the QuikTrip, make a left on Hemphill. I'll meet you on that street."

"Alright."

"How long it'll take you to get there?"

"I'm about to get off the freeway."

"What you driving?"

"A black Suburban."

"A'ight."

At the meeting spot, she pulled over on the side of the road and turned her headlights off. The neighborhood was quiet. Her mind was anything but. She didn't have to wait long before a pair of headlights pulled up behind her. She prayed it wasn't the police; they were known to have a heavy presence in the area. When the headlights went off, she blew out a sigh of relief when she saw that it was a Honda parked behind her.

The driver exited the vehicle and walked to her side of the car. In the side mirror, she saw that Boom's contact was black, a little chubby, and his hands were empty. When he was close enough, he stood a few feet away from her door and peered inside. Asha stared back at him.

The man was young, in his mid-thirties. He wore black scrubs with an emblem on the breast that Asha recognized as Carter BloodCare's logo. She wondered how Boom had made acquaintances with him. She wondered how he was able to sneak blood out of his place of business. But most of all, she wanted to hurry and complete this transaction. It would take another forty minutes to get back to the animal hospital.

The man's eyes moved from Asha to the door of the SUV. He grimaced as his attention returned to her.

He said, "This the real deal, huh?"

She nodded numbly.

"Is he gon' be alright?" the stranger asked. "He got hit bad?"

"Yeah," Asha said. "Bad enough. You got the blood?"

"Yeah, yeah. Lemme go get it."

He returned to his car and came back with some sort of high-tech cooler. "You want me to put it in the back?"

"No," Asha said, worried about it getting jostled. "I'ma keep it up front with me."

"Okay. I'll bring it around."

He rounded the car and hesitated when he opened the passenger door. "*Damn.* Somebody got killed in here?"

"You asking too many questions," Asha replied. "Just leave it there."

"I'm just saying... This a lot of fucking blood."

"Just leave it." Her eyes were as cold as winter.

The man placed the cooler on the bloody seat and closed the door. Asha reached to the backseat for Slimey's Gucci bag.

"How much I owe you for this?" she asked.

Instead of a response, the man asked her, "Why you ain't take him to the hospital? Who y'all know that's gon' do a blood transfusion?"

"You need to chill with all these questions."

But he couldn't help himself. "It's you, ain't it? You Brionna..."

"How much do I owe you," she asked slowly, her eyes growing more fierce.

He shook his head. "Nothing. Me and Boom worked this out a couple of years ago. He took care of something for me, and I owe him a favor. This is how he wanted me to pay him back, if he ever needed it. But that nigga so hard, I didn't think there would come a day when I'd have to repay him."

"Alright, well I ain't tryna be rude, but I need to hurry up and get this back to him. I'm sure Boom will call and thank you, if he pull through."

"Alright. It's cool. Tell that nigga I'm praying for him."

The blood thief backed away in time to avoid getting his toes run over as she drove away.

CHAPTER 29

BACK AT THE animal hospital, Asha found the door to the surgical room unit. She walked inside and found Doc hard at work. The sight of Boom on the lift table, naked, with tubes shoved down his throat, made her knees buckle. The vet looked her way before returning his attention to the hole he was focused on. His face was dotted with sweat, his gloves covered with blood.

"Got what I need?" he asked.

Asha nodded, walking to him on weary legs. Her mind was frazzled. She didn't think she could endure more mental trauma. She approached the table and stared at her man. Boom was positioned on his side. His eyes were closed, his skin ashen. He was connected to a breathing machine that hummed like a generator. Asha knew the machine was responsible for his chest rising and falling at steady intervals. She'd been in enough hospital rooms to know something was missing. Boom should've had electrodes stuck to his skin, connected to an EKG monitor that would display his vital signs.

"How's it going?" she asked. Sometime in the wee hours of the morning, her voice had become hoarse and raspy.

"*It's going*," Doc said with a sigh. "I think I almost got this one..."

Asha put the cooler on the floor and moved to his side of the table. She saw that he'd made an incision on Boom's back that was almost two inches long. Surgical retractors held the skin and muscle open, while Doc dug in the wound with a pair of oddly shaped forceps. Blood steadily oozed from the hole. The sight made Asha cringe. Outside of TV, she'd never seen surgery before. She desperately wanted to believe the vet knew what he was doing, but doubt gripped her like a straitjacket.

She was more stunned than relieved when she heard him murmur, "*Here we go...*" a moment before slowly withdrawing the forceps. When the tip of the tool emerged from Boom's skin, she saw a battered bullet gripped in the teeth.

Doc dropped the bullet on a tray and reached for a wash bottle that had a curved, pointed spout. He squirted distilled water in the wound and reached for the forceps again. He returned to the hole and resumed digging.

"Gotta make sure there are no fragments," he explained. "Don't wanna leave anything behind..."

Asha couldn't pull her eyes away. She remained frozen in place until he was done cleaning the wound, suturing the layer of muscle tissue, and finally stitching up the skin.

"Alrighty," he said. "One down."

He taped a layer of gauze over the cut and then rolled Boom to his back. He left the patient and went to wash his hands. He then began to rummage through one of the drawers near the sink. He shook his head and checked a few cabinets on both sides of the room.

Asha knew she could offer no insight, but she had to ask him, "What are you looking for?"

"A blood warmer."

Asha expected something like a microwave, but when he found what he was looking for, she saw that the device was about the size of a blood pressure monitor. He took it the table and secured it to the IV pole. He walked to the cooler and knelt to inspect the contents.

"Perfect," he said, selecting one of the bags. He hung the blood and connected the tubes. One line fed blood into the warmer. Another line ran from the warmer to an IV, providing Boom with the rich oil of life. Asha was enthralled, as if she was watching a magic show.

When he was done, he said, "Okay, now let me get to this other bullet. The X-ray showed it's stuck in his rib. It actually cracked the rib, so I may have a little trouble getting it out."

Asha thought that was a horrible predicament.

But Doc said, "That's actually a good thing. If it had went through the rib, it could've hit his heart or lungs. You said he was in the car when he got shot?"

She nodded. "Yeah. On the driver's side."

"The door probably saved his life," Doc said, examining the bullet hole. "The door slowed the bullet down, otherwise his rib wouldn't have stopped it. The first bullet I took out did way more damage, but this rib will take a while to heal. If Boom survives, it'll be weeks before he's back to his old self."

"You, you don't think he'll make it?"

The vet had returned to the sink to wash his hands again and get another pair of gloves. With his back to her, he said, "Honestly, I don't know. I told you I'm not an anesthesiologist. I think I got it right when I put him under, but until I take him off the vent and he wakes up and breathes on his own, I won't be sure."

Asha didn't know how to respond to that.

She remained quiet for the next thirty minutes, while the vet removed the second bullet and stitched everything up. When he was ready to remove the breathing tube, Asha subconsciously held her breath, waiting to see if Boom would survive without it. The intubation tube was long enough to slide the full length of his throat, all the way to his lungs. Removing it looked painful. She was grateful that at the moment, Boom couldn't feel a thing.

When Doc got the tube out, nothing happened at first. A moment later, Boom coughed and then filled his lungs with oxygen. With his first exhalation, he coughed again. His first breaths were short and ragged. Asha knew that if he had been connected to an EKG, the readings would be going crazy. But her man proved to be a warrior. Gradually his breathing stabilized.

Doc blew out a sigh of relief. He replaced the breathing tube with an oxygen mask that was connected to a portable tank. "Okay. That's the best we could've hoped for. But we're not out of the woods yet. I won't know if I got the anesthesia right until he wakes up."

"How, how long is that supposed to take?"

"I hope he'll be awake within the hour." He checked his watch. "But I won't be around to see it, and neither will you."

Asha didn't think she'd heard him right. "*What? Why not?*"

"I have to open up in an hour. That gives me enough time to move him and run home to shower."

Asha's frown deepened. "What do you mean, *move him?*"

"I have another exam room, way in back," he said. "I'll lock the door and make sure no one goes back there. I might need this area, if someone brings a large animal today."

Just when she was ready to give this man his props, he reminded her how horrible this whole experience had been. "*You wanna leave him back there by hisself?* What if something goes wrong? What if he doesn't wake up?"

"I'll check on him," the vet promised.

"I'll stay with him," Asha decided.

"No, ma'am, you will not. I just told you my employees will be here soon. I don't want them to see Boom or your *bloody, bullet-riddled* car."

"I'll switch cars and come back."

"Unless you bring a sick horse with you, you have no reason to be here." He stopped moving long enough to look her in the eyes. "You said Boom told you to call me because he trusted me. Now it's time for you to trust me. Go home, get some rest. I'll call you when I have an update.

"In the meantime, you might need to come up with more money to pay for this. I don't know how much you gave me earlier, but I'm charging thirty thousand for the surgery. I'll need ten more for caring for him while he's here. After I count what you've already paid, I'll let you know how short you are."

Asha began to tremble with rage. At this point, she felt like this man was purposefully goading her into taking his life. Or maybe she was the one who was wrong. Perhaps, given the circumstances, the vet had been as professional and meticulous as possible. Should she fault him for expecting compensation? Asha realized her emotions might be causing her to react the way she did.

She pursed her lips and told him, "*Fine.*"

She returned to the table and placed a hand on Boom's cheek. She bent and kissed him softly.

She told him, "I love you, baby. Everything will be okay. I'll see you soon."

Walking away from him was one of the hardest things she ever had to do. She looked back before exiting the building. Doc was busy cleaning up and collecting his supplies. He stopped for a moment to see her out. When he closed the door, she heard him lock it this time.

PART FOUR
NONCOMMITTAL

CHAPTER 30

BEFORE HEADING HOME, Asha stopped at one of their safehouses on the northside. She left the bloody SUV there and took off in a black Mustang. She knew Boom wouldn't approve of the move. If she was with him, he would've left the SUV ablaze in a field somewhere. But Asha would need another driver to assist with that. She had a couple of people she could call, but she had more pressing matters to attend to.

When she finally made it home, the sun was peaking over the horizon. So far, she'd been awake for 24 hours. She parked in the garage and was overcome by a sense of emptiness when she entered the house. It was an emotion she'd never felt there, ever since she traded in her old life for a wild ride on Boom's murder train.

She went to the bathroom and stripped out of her bloody clothes. She made sure to bring a trash bag with her, so she could dispose of everything she had on, just as Boom would want her to. Standing nude before the bathroom mirror, she saw that the stress from the previous night had taken a toll on her appearance. She looked haggard, her hair unkempt. Dark bags under her eyes aged her five years or more. Blood had soaked through her clothes and stained her skin. She looked like she'd murdered a whole house full of people.

She hadn't cried in hours, but in the shower, she allowed herself to break down one last time. Her tears were lost in the spray of water that washed away the blood but not the memories from last night. When she left the tub, her eyes were dry, and her resolve had been fortified. Rather than head to bed for much needed rest, she went to the bedroom and found one of her burner phones. It was 7:12 a.m. She knew her cousin wasn't prone to rising this early, but she made the call anyway.

The phone rang four times before Tristan answered with a groggy, "Who's this?"

"It's me, Asha."

"Damn, cuzzo. What time is it? Why you calling so early?"

"I'm 'bout to come see you," she said, "in about an hour. I need you to do something for me before I get there."

"A'ight. What's up?"

"I need you to make some calls and see if anyone heard anything about Solomon and Boom. Some shit went down last night. I need to know what the streets are saying."

"What's wrong? What happened?"

"That's what I need you to find out."

"Ain't you with Boom? Why don't you just ask him?"

Only two people in Asha's family knew that she and Boom were a couple, and on the streets, she was infamously known as *Brionna*. Her sister Gloria was one of those people. Tristan was the other.

"I'm not with Boom," she said vaguely. "Can you make some calls and see what you can find out?"

"I don't know nobody who would know nothing about them – not nobody who'd be up this early."

Asha knew that wasn't true. Tristan was a drug dealer, and his drug dealing cohorts were available 24 hours a day.

"Don't forget what I did for you, when Mr. Brown and them was on yo ass."

She'd never brought up the blood trail she'd left behind to save her cousin's life. Tristan knew that if she was calling in the favor now, this must be serious.

"A'ight," he said. "I'll see what I can find out."

Asha returned to the bathroom and examined her nude physique again. Rather than haggard, she thought she looked as fierce as ever. She walked into the closet in search of a suitable disguise. She opted for a gang girl persona – baggy jeans, a large tee shirt and white sneakers. Back in the bathroom, she tied her hair back and put on a wig that gave her braids down past her shoulders.

She returned to the closet and grabbed Boom's tattoo kit. The temporary tats would hold firm, even after a shower. She applied a few to her arms and an ostentatious one that read "Fuck You" on her neck. She added a gold grill, a couple of gold necklaces and completed her outfit with a double pistol holster. She stuffed identical 9mm's in the holsters that fit snugly against her ribs.

Before leaving the house, she checked to see if she'd missed a call or message from Doc.

She had not.

CHAPTER 31

TRISTAN LIVED IN an apartment complex on the south side. Asha parked in front of his building and called him to meet her, rather than leave her car. Out of concern for his safety, she didn't want anyone to see him in cahoots with the tatted-up gang girl. There was no telling what she'd get into after she spoke to him.

She watched her cousin emerge from his apartment and make his way down the stairs. Tristan was a caramel-colored pretty boy. He wore his hair long and had a mess of tattoos. Wearing a tee shirt and shorts, most were visible on his arms and neck. He found Asha's expression unreadable when he locked eyes with her through the Charger's windshield. He got in the car and did a double take when he took in her appearance.

"What's up, cuz? You good?" His eyes narrowed as he looked her up and down. "You got all these tats since my party?" The obscenity on her neck gave him the most pause. "What you do that shit for?"

Asha trusted her cousin, but until she got to the bottom of the mystery she was embroiled in, she could trust no one. Rather than tell him the tats weren't real, she simply ignored him.

"You found something out?" she asked.

He nodded, still trying to come to terms with her appearance. "They say Solomon got killed, Boom too," he said solemnly. "You ain't tell me yo nigga was dead..."

Asha did not react to that news, though her mind was racing. She quickly decided that if the hood thought Boom was dead, it would be beneficial to let them keep thinking that. His enemies might let their guard down.

When she didn't respond, Tristan said, "You alright?"

She shook her head. Boom's prognosis was still undetermined, so it didn't take too much acting to pull off the forlorn look she wore.

"Naw, I'm not good." She looked him in the eyes. "I need to know who did it."

Tristan's mouth went dry. This was not the same girl he used to go to the community pool with when they were younger. Some of his earliest fights were with boys who thought dunking Asha in the water was an appropriate way to express their interest.

"I don't know who did it – not for sure," he said. "But it don't look like Boom was the target. They saying that whoever killed Solomon did it 'cause he was trying to kill them first. This shit all started after Mr. Brown got killed. Most niggas was okay with taking whatever slice of the pie they had, but Solomon wanted it all. He got a little hit list together and hired somebody to take out the competition. Nobody I talked to knew he hired Boom – until now. Since him and Solomon got killed at the same time, people are saying Boom must've been the hitter."

Asha remained emotionless, though her intuition was blaring once again. This was the same story Slimey had told. Solomon had sworn that he didn't run his mouth, but he must have told *someone* what his plans were.

She told Tristan, "You said you don't know for sure who did it. Who you *think* did it?"

"Cuz..." He rubbed his forehead anxiously. "I ain't tryna send you after somebody who didn't do that shit. It could've been any of them niggas on Solomon's hit list."

"Well, who they saying was on Solomon's list?"

"All the big timers," he replied. "Lynx, Slim, Slimey – but that nigga dead. Um, Pacman was on there too..."

Asha watched his eyes, wondering if he was holding back. It didn't appear that he was.

"Slim and Lynx the only ones still alive," Tristan continued. "It was prolly one of them. If I had to guess, I'd say Slim – but maybe it wasn't. I know you feel like you gotta do what you gotta do for Boom, but killing some innocent niggas ain't gon' solve nothing."

She asked him, "Are you cool with them niggas or something?"

He quickly shook his head. "Naw. Hell, naw, cuz. You know I would never fuck with nobody in Mr. Brown's crew after that shit went down. Me and Slim ain't cool. We ain't nothing. I don't even know that nigga. I don't know Lynx, either."

"Good. Tell me where I can find them."

Tristan shook his head again, grudgingly accepting that he could do nothing to come between Asha and her vengeance. "I don't know where them niggas at," he told her. "I know you don't believe me, but I swear I don't."

Asha did believe him. "Well, who you think I should ask?"

"Fuck," Tristan said with a sigh. "Asha, I really don't want you to hem none of my niggas up over this shit."

"If one of yo niggas know where Slim and Lynx at, it'd be better if I'm the one who asked them. If you start asking them kind of questions, people gon' point they finger at you when they end up dead."

Tristan frowned and blew out another sigh. "Why don't you talk to Perm," he suggested. "That nigga know everything."

Asha had never heard the name before. "Where can I find him?"

"He got a shooting gallery on St Louis."

"You got the address?"

"Naw, but it's right on the corner of St Louis and Butler. It's a blue house, you can't miss it. If it's a gray Accord in the driveway, that mean Perm there."

"Alright. Thanks."

Tristan's eyes softened. "Say, cuz, I know you know how to handle yourself, but you should let me ride with you. These niggas you after done already took out Solomon, and that nigga was untouchable. You gon' need somebody to watch yo back."

"Didn't you tell me Courtney was pregnant again?"

"Yeah, but–"

"Ain't no buts, Tristan. That girl popping out babies as fast as you can get 'em in there. If you wanna play family guy and shit, that's cool. But you need to stay in yo lane. It'll be hard to raise them kids from prison. Truth be told, you need to leave that dope game alone. What's gon' happen to Courtney, if you get arrested?"

"I know you ain't lecturing me while you out there killing folks."

"I ain't got no responsibilities. That's the difference. If I was in yo shoes, best believe my ass would be working at Home Depot. I'll holler at you later."

Tristan looked like he wanted to say something else, but he knew it wouldn't help. He got out of the car and left Asha to pursue her own path in life, while he contemplated his.

CHAPTER 32

PERM'S *SHOOTING GALLERY* had nothing to do with recreational target practice. It was a place junkies went, primarily heroin addicts, to inject their poison, zone out, and enjoy their high in peace. Perm profited from his customers by selling drugs and charging them to remain there until their high wore off.

Asha had no idea what Perm looked like, but she saw that his Honda Accord was parked in the driveway, so she knew she was watching the right house, and her person of interest was inside. She did not like conducting stakeouts, but the stakes for this one were so high, even her lack of sleep didn't dull her vigilance.

At 11 o'clock, she'd been watching the house for three hours. In that time, she'd seen half a dozen customers visit the house. A couple of them left within minutes, but most remained there. Asha had only seen one woman stay for over an hour and then leave, her eyes more zombified than before she entered. None of the customers spotted Asha, parked in front of a vacant house down the street. If any of the neighbors had noticed her, they weren't curious enough to inquire about why she was there.

When the owner of the illicit business finally emerged from the front door, Asha sat up in her seat. She noticed Perm did not have long hair, let alone a perm, and he didn't feel the need to make his remaining customers vacate the home before he left. The man was tall and lanky, in his late forties. Even from a distance, Asha could see the pockmarks on his cheeks. Perm hopped into his Honda and backed out of the driveway. Asha gave him a little room before she got on his tail.

She followed him for twenty minutes. Thankfully Perm only made one stop, in an apartment complex not far from his dope spot. He disappeared inside a first-floor apartment and exited less than five minutes later. Asha suspected he had bought more heroin to resale to his customers. She hoped he wouldn't return to the shooting gallery. If he did, she knew he'd be there for hours. She'd have to enter the house and expose herself to witnesses in order to interrogate him. This time, luck was on her side.

Perm drove to a different neighborhood and pulled into the driveway of a modest home. Asha drove slowly past in time to see him enter the house. There were no other cars in the driveway, no toys or bikes in the front yard. Asha suspected Perm was a bachelor, and this was the best time to intercept him.

She parked around the corner and walked casually to an alley than ran through the block, behind Perm's house. Boom had taught her to never consider entering a home until she'd gathered intel on all of the exits. The alley was cleaner than most but still not a place you could drive a car through. Asha suspected snakes and rats were hiding in the overgrown grass and dense shrubbery, but she didn't hesitate when she reached the entrance. A few moments later, she had disappeared from the street view.

When she reached the back of the target's house, her element of surprise was thwarted when Perm opened the back door, and a menacing pit bull came running out. After her last run-in with a ferocious canine, Asha was understandably leery. She froze in place, concealed by the overgrowth, but the dog's powerful senses were not limited to sight. It sniffed around the backyard, relieved itself on its favorite pissing tree and then sniffed the air again. Its massive head swung in Asha's direction, and she would swear they locked eyes. The dog charged the fence, no more than three feet away from her, and began barking madly.

Perm had closed the back door by then, but he was close enough to open it immediately. He stared at his dog and then in Asha's direction. His eyes narrowed, but Asha knew he couldn't see her. The dog continued to sound the alarm. Now it stood on its hind legs, with both front paws on the fence. Asha remained still. Her eyes moved from the dog to the back door, which was empty now. A few seconds later, Perm appeared again, toting a shotgun this time. He raised it into firing position, toting it at hip level, and walked slowly towards the gate.

Asha had no idea if he'd loaded the weapon with buckshot or slugs, but if he used the weapon for home protection, she banked on buckshot. Things would end badly if she was wrong, but if she waited any longer, the buckshot could be just as deadly.

She reached under her shirt and withdrew both pistols. Perm stopped in his tracks when he heard her cock them. Before stepping into view, she announced her presence.

"*Don't move! I got the drop on you!*"

She stepped forward with one gun aimed at the dog and the other pointed at Perm's chest.

"You know you can't do shit with that shotgun from way over there!" She had to yell to be heard over the barking. "But I can kill you and yo dog right now! I ain't here to rob you!" she promised. "I'm just here to talk. Come get this dog, before I kill 'em!"

"Who are you?" Perm yelled back.

"I ain't nobody! I just need yo help with something! Come get this dog! I swear I'ma 'bout to kill this motherfucker, then I'ma have to kill yo ass too!" When he didn't respond, she shouted, "A'ight. Fuck it!"

"*Wait! Stop! I'ma get 'em! I'ma get 'em!*"

"Put that shotgun down first!"

The dog was so incensed by then, it was trying to jump the gate. Asha could not explain where she found the courage to hold her ground.

Perm put his shotgun on the ground and came closer to retrieve his dog. His eyes remained on Asha the whole time. He grabbed the dog by the collar and fought to drag it away from the gate.

"You got somewhere to chain him up?" Asha wanted to know.

Perm shot her a look of disgust rather than respond. He wasn't able to turn the dog away from her, but he managed to pull it to one of the trees. With his free hand, he found a chain lying in the grass and affixed it to the dog's collar. When he let go, the pit charged the gate again. This time, its progress was painfully halted by the chain going taut.

"Stay right there!" Asha shouted. "I'm finna jump this gate! Keep yo hands where I can see 'em! Don't reach for that fucking chain!"

Perm continued to give her as much attitude as a defeated man could, but he didn't move when Asha jumped the gate, even though she wasn't able to keep her gun pointed at him the whole time. Once on the other side, the dog went from furious to ballistic. But by then, it was all for naught. There was no way it could accomplish its primary duty – to protect the man who fed and cared for it.

"Alright," Asha said, her gun still on Perm. "Let's go inside and talk. I take it ain't nobody else home."

"Naw ain't nobody in there," Perm said, heading for the back door.

When they entered the house, he took a seat at the kitchen table. Asha closed the door, surprised by how compliant he had become. She sat across from him.

He told her, "You ain't gotta point that gun at me. I know why you're here, and I know who you are."

She lowered her weapon but didn't return it to the holster. "Who do you think I am?"

"You Brionna, ain't you? Look, I'm sorry about what happened to your man, but you ain't got no right to come to my house like this, fucking with my dog and shit. I know you Brionna, 'cause you and Boom just the same – think just 'cause I got my ear to the street, I know everything y'all wanna know. Last time yo man was here, he woke me up with a sledgehammer in his hand, talking 'bout he was gon' fuck me up if I didn't help him find you. He did something to my dog, too. Put him to sleep. I know who you are. You ain't gotta say it…"

Asha was so taken aback, she couldn't have responded if she wanted to. Boom never told her about this man, but Perm knew Boom's tactics very well. The fact that she'd circumstantially found herself interrogating the same man Boom once interrogated was surreal.

"Alright, well, if you know why I'm here," she said, "tell me what I need to know, and I'll leave."

He shrugged. "Sorry, but I don't know who killed Solomon and Boom."

She shook her head. "You know Boom wouldn't leave without getting more than that, so why you think I would?"

She reached into her pocket and produced a fold of bills. She placed it on the table. "If you want that, you gotta tell me something. Otherwise I'ma have to do something to make sure you really don't know nothing. I already know how much you love that damn dog, so that's the first thing I'ma shoot."

The look in her eyes told him she wasn't taking no for an answer. Or maybe threatening the dog did the trick. Whatever the case, Perm's nostrils flared. He sneered at her, shook his head, sighed, and then he started talking.

He didn't know much more than Tristan did. He knew Solomon had a hit list, and he knew Slim and Lynx were on it. He didn't know Boom was the hitter Solomon had hired until word got out about the shooting. But he had one piece of new information that piqued Asha's interest.

"You know Slim was fucking Solomon's ol' lady…"

Asha tried to play it cool. "No shit?"

"Yup. They been fucking for damn near a year. If I was betting on it, I'd say Slim the one who pulled the trigger.

That woulda got Solomon back for trying to kill him *and* freed up the gal, so they could be together. That's a win-win for Slim. Niggas kill they woman's other nigga all the time. Don't matter if Solomon had her first. That love shit is a strong emotion."

Asha nodded. "Okay. The only thing left is for you to tell me where Slim lay his head."

He shook his head. "Now you trying to get me killed for real. If it ever got out that I'm the one who told you, them niggas ain't just gon' kill me. They'll do me like what happened to BD."

Perm knew a lot about the streets, but he did not know he was sitting across from the person who had shot BD's dick off.

"Did anything you ever told Boom ever come back on you?" she asked.

He considered that. "Naw. That nigga ain't never ran his mouth."

"Then why you think that's something you need to worry about? Me and Boom the same – ain't that what you said?"

Solomon brought a hand to his face and rubbed his lips, and then he told her what she wanted to know.

CHAPTER 33

FIVE MINUTES LATER, Asha was behind the wheel of the Charger again. She checked her phone. Still no messages or missed calls from Doc. She wanted to believe that was a good sign. If Boom had died, the vet would've called to let her know. But he said he'd call when Boom woke up. Did this mean Boom was struggling to overcome the anesthesia?

She cursed Doc under her breath and started the car. She considered heading straight to the animal hospital to give the vet a piece of her mind. She decided to give him a little more time to do the right thing, the courteous thing.

In the meantime, she had bigger fish to fry.

CHAPTER 34

ASHA DROVE TO the address Perm had given her and found Slim's home in a nice, mostly black neighborhood. It was an impressive, two-story house with a manicured lawn and beautiful shade trees in the front yard. The neighborhood was so nice, Asha didn't think she could conduct a proper stakeout in broad daylight. Fortunately, she didn't have to. She'd only been on Slim's street for ten minutes before four men emerged from the house. Before they piled into a new Escalade, Asha spotted her next target.

Perm had given her a description of Slim, but it wasn't needed. At 6'5", Slim was the tallest in the crew and also the thinnest. He was handsome, but Asha didn't think he was handsome enough for Solomon's woman to risk it all to be with him. Then again, looks were not always the primary draw when it came to these types of men. With Slimey and Pacman out of the picture, Slim was the last lieutenant left standing in Mr. Brown's organization. He was certainly a millionaire, like Solomon, and he had plenty of street cred.

The moment Asha laid eyes on him, she knew Slim wasn't the person who shot Solomon and Boom. She wasn't sure how she knew, but she did. That knowledge did not alter her plans to murder this man. Even if Slim didn't personally pull the trigger, that didn't mean he wasn't responsible. To get Solomon's woman all to himself, he could've paid to have it done.

Asha gave the Cadillac as much leeway as possible, but in the quiet neighborhood, she didn't feel confident about tailing them. She liked her chances a lot better when they turned onto a main throughfare a few minutes later. She followed the Escalade to an apartment complex where a party was in full swing. There were so many people outside, it was hard to tell which resident was hosting the get-together. Someone had brought a few barbecue pits and set up shop in one of the handicap parking spaces. The main source of music came from that area. More music blared from the speakers of some of the cars parked nearby.

With so many people outside and some sitting in their cars, Asha felt comfortable enough to park and watch the scene. But she remained wary. It appeared this party was attended by multiple members of Mr. Brown's organization – which could be considered *Slim's* organization at this point. That meant everyone there was potentially her enemy. If Perm had backstabbed her and gave them a heads up, she might not make it out of there alive.

Asha kept her eyes on Slim when he exited the Escalade. The drug lord mingled with the crowd jovially. Everyone he passed stopped what they were doing to dap him up and speak to him. He was definitely the most important person there. His underlings had to pay homage.

As she surveilled the party, Asha began to doubt her chances of catching Slim alone. If he was constantly surrounded by his goons, it was unlikely she'd be able to put him down without bodying everyone inside the house. She wondered what advice Boom would give her. Thinking of him, she checked her phone. Still no word from Doc. Annoyed, she called the only number she had for the veterinarian.

No answer.

Slim and his crew remained at the party for over an hour. When they left, Asha followed them back to his house. By then, it was 3 pm. There were too many neighbors out and about for her to post up like she wanted to, so she didn't pull over. She made a left at the next intersection and headed out of the neighborhood. She could pick up where she left off after nightfall.

CHAPTER 35

AN HOUR LATER, she pulled into a parking spot in front of the animal hospital in Cedar Hill. She noticed the side gate was open and debated if she should head back there, to the last place she'd seen Boom. She decided against it. She didn't want to be *completely* rachet at Doc's place of business. But then she glanced down at her arms and remembered her tattoos. Without a bottle of baby oil, there was no way to remove them.

She knew that most of Doc's customers were probably white, cowboy or farmer types. With her gang girl disguise, Asha was anything but. Due to her appearance, rachetness was unavoidable. But as a concession, she removed the gold grill from her mouth before exiting her car.

Inside the main building, there was only one person in the reception area. The woman was understandably taken aback when Asha sauntered through the doors. She couldn't tear her eyes away from the large "Fuck you," on her neck. Even still, she was professional enough to offer a courteous greeting, when Asha approached the counter.

"Hi, may I help you?"

"Yeah. I need to talk to..." Asha suddenly realized she didn't know Doc's real name. "The vet," she offered. "I need to talk to the vet."

"Umm, okay..." The woman's eyes narrowed. "What can I do for you?"

"I need to talk to him about my horse," Asha said. "I need to talk to him *personally*. He knows what this is about."

"We, um... We don't have any horses here right now. Are you sure you're at the right hospital?"

"I'm at the right place. Could you go get him? He'll know what I'm talking about."

"Ma'am," the woman persisted, "if you brought a horse here, I would've been the one to check him in. I don't believe–"

"I just told you the vet knows what I'm talking about. Can you go get him, or do you want me to go in there and find him?"

Flustered, the woman reached for the phone. A moment later, she spoke into the receiver, her eyes on Asha the whole time. "Dr. Moretti, there's a woman here who says she wants to check on her horse... Yes, I told her we don't have any horses here today. She's very insistent about wanting to speak with you. She says you know what horse she's talking about. Okay. I'm sorry to bother you. Thank you."

She hung up and told Asha, "He'll be right here."

Asha stood there for two minutes. The receptionist stared at her the whole time, not bothering to find something to busy herself with. Doc finally emerged from the door behind her. He frowned when he saw Asha and then made his expression neutral when his receptionist looked back at him.

"Hi, how can I help you?" he asked.

Asha hoped he'd step outside with her. She didn't know how to play this off with the woman watching them. "I'm here about my horse."

"Are you Mrs. Ward?" Doc asked. "I believe I spoke with you last night."

"Yeah. I'm Mrs. Ward."

"You said your horse is not mobile, and I told you I'd call you after we close today and see if I can come to your place to check on him. We close at five." He checked his watch. "That's about an hour from now. I'll call you at five, before I head your way."

"No," Asha said, shaking her head. "I need to know about my horse *now*."

"I'm sure your horse is *fine*," Doc said, frowning again. "I will call you at five, and we can discuss this then."

Asha's nostrils flared. She knew what he was trying to tell her, but she didn't want to leave without seeing Boom. "Fine," she said. "I expect to hear from you at five."

She turned and left the building.

To kill time, she found a Dairy Queen restaurant not far from the animal hospital. She remembered enjoying their chicken tender basket when she was younger. But when she pulled out of the drive through and found a parking spot, the food didn't look appetizing at all. She forced herself to eat it anyway. She was already suffering from lack of sleep. If she added lack of nutrients to the mix, she may not have the energy to accomplish tonight's mission.

She was still in the parking lot when Doc called at 5:10.

"Hello."

He told her, "Give my employees a chance to clear out, and you can come back in about fifteen minutes."

"Alright. Do you want me to park out front or–"

"No. You can go to the building we were in last night."

"Okay. Is Boom alright?"

"Yes. He's awake, but he may be drowsy. He's heavily medicated. He was awake the last time I checked on him, but I'm not sure if he went back to sleep."

"Why didn't you call to tell me how he's been doing? You said you would call me when he woke up."

"I'm sorry. I've been busy."

"What do you mean you been busy? It only takes a minute to pick up the phone."

"I said I was sorry. I've been under a lot of stress to care for Boom and make sure none of my staff knows he's here. I've given him the best care I can. I'm not used to giving a report to someone who is not under my care. But I did plan to call you today at closing time, even if you *didn't* show up at my office. That was very unprofessional, by the way. I have to ask you to never do that again."

Asha was ready to blow a fuse. She wondered if Boom was well enough to survive on his own, if she decided to return to the clinic and put a bullet in Doc's head.

She told him, "Whatever, man. I'll be there in fifteen minutes."

CHAPTER 36

BACK AT THE animal hospital, only Doc's Mercedes remained in the parking lot. Asha drove to the back of the building, as instructed, and parked near the door she exited last night. She found the door locked. She knocked, and Doc came to open it for her. When they were face to face, he looked her up and down and shook his head. He turned and led her down one of the halls.

"If you were gonna come here during business hours," he commented, without looking back, "the least you could've done was dress appropriately. You do not look like someone who either owns a horse or could afford to care for one."

Oh my God, you better shut the fuck up, Asha thought. If the vet made it down the hallway without getting punched in the back of the head, she'd consider that her good deed for the day.

The vet stopped at the door of another exam room and pushed it open. "I'm gonna head back to the main building," he said. "I'll be back in a little bit."

When he walked away, Asha stepped inside. She shuddered inwardly when she saw her man lying on the same lift table as last night. The room was small and dimly lit. There were no windows or decorations on the walls. There was a sink in one corner but no bathroom. It was not the kind of place you'd want to find your loved one who had a serious medical condition. It looked like the kind of place a third world country might stuff a terminally ill patient, to clear a room for someone who had a chance for survival.

But Boom was not dead. He looked comfortable, with a blanket pulled up to his chest. His breathing was normal. When Asha stepped closer to the table, his eyes fluttered open, and his head rolled her way. He didn't register any emotion. Asha reached to hold his hand. His grip was not strong, but she felt his fingers move to hold her back.

She smiled wistfully. Her eyes filled with tears.

"If you wanted to take some time off work," she joked, "you could've just said so. You ain't have to do all this."

His lips curved slightly into a smile. That was the best thing Asha had seen in years.

"How you feeling?" she asked. "Can you talk?"

He nodded and then proved he could still communicate. "I ain't great, but I'm making it."

His voice was faint and raspy. He took a deep breath to recuperate from the effort it took him to speak those few words.

"What about you?" he asked. "How you holding up?"

She shook her head. "Not good. I miss you. And I'm sick of this fucking vet." She checked to make sure he wasn't behind her. "I think I might have to do him when this is over."

Boom chuckled and then grimaced. His grip on her hand tightened. "Don't, don't make me laugh," he said, panting slightly. "Shit hurt."

Asha's eyes filled with concern. "I'm sorry. But I'm serious. That nigga get on my damn nerves."

"What he do that got you so riled up?"

"I don't like the way he talk to me. *Fucking rude.*"

Boom's smile was weak, but it did Asha's heart good to see it. "You said the same thing about me when we first met," he recalled. "Matter of fact, you called me an asshole."

Asha remembered that. She could not remember the moment her feelings about him changed.

"What difference it make if he rude" Boom asked, "as long as he get the job done? Who else you know can do what he do?"

Outside of a hospital, Asha could think of no one.

"I don't like how he was talking about money, while you was in there bleeding to death," she said, not willing to let Doc off the hook.

Boom smacked his lips. "I know you ain't mad at him for wanting to get paid, as much as you been paper chasing."

"Alright," Asha said with a roll of her eyes. "I hear you. I guess I'll let him make it."

Boom nodded. His eyes narrowed as he looked her up and down. "What's up with that shit you got on? What you been up to?"

"Trying to get to the bottom of this," she replied, "find out who shot you."

Boom frowned. "I don't like the idea of you out there by yourself. What'd you do today?"

Asha looked back again and decided to close the door. She returned to her man and reached to hold his hand again.

"I didn't do nothing you wouldn't do, if I was the one who was laid up..."

She told him everything she'd done that day, starting with her call to Tristan and ending with following Slim and his crew back to his home. Boom did not interrupt her while she was speaking. When she was done, he asked about something she'd said midway through her spiel.

"You said Slim ain't the one who shot me?"

She shook her head. "Naw. It ain't him."

"How you know? You know who shot me?"

"No. If I knew who shot you, I wouldn't be doing all this."

Boom asked the obvious question. "Well, if you don't know who shot me, how you know it wasn't Slim?"

She shook her head and shrugged. "I don't know. But I know it wasn't him. It's just, I mean... I don't really know how to explain it. It's just a feeling I got."

Boom watched her eyes and decided to let it go for now. Asha wasn't surprised when he told her, "You need to chill; lay low till I get better. You don't need to be out there wilding by yourself. For all we know, whoever shot me is gunning for you too."

"If they are, don't you think it make sense for me to get them first? Ain't that what you would do?"

"Yeah, but you ain't got me with you to help. You ain't got nobody. We can take care of this when I get back on my feet."

"Boom, I don't think this is a good time for me to lay low. Everybody think you dead. This the perfect time to go after 'em."

"You ain't listening to me. I'm telling you to wait. You out there making moves by yourself – I'm 100 percent against that shit."

The frustration in his eyes was exacerbated by the pain it was causing him to speak so forcefully. Asha didn't want to tell him she'd fall back, when she had no intention of doing so, so she didn't say anything at all.

"Girl, did you hear what I said?"

As much as she hated the vet, Asha was grateful when he knocked on the door and then opened it. They both looked his way.

"Hey," Doc said, "I'm sorry to interrupt, but I have to head home for a little bit. My wife gives me a little leeway, when it comes to stuff like this, but I have to have dinner with the family. I don't have *any* leeway, as far as that's concerned. I'll be back afterwards. I might spend the night here. I gotta lock up, till I get back."

"Okay," Asha said. She kissed Boom on the side of the mouth and then released his hand. His eyes remained glued to hers as she backed away from the table. "I'll see you later," she said.

She could tell Boom had more to say, but he didn't ask Doc to give them more time together. "Remember what I told you," he said, before she disappeared through the doorway.

She looked back and nodded, once again noncommittal. "I love you, baby. I'll see you later."

She hurried to tear her eyes away from his. Even from his weakened position, Boom's willpower was strong. But, for now at least, hers was much stronger.

PART FIVE
REAL TEARS

CHAPTER 37

WITH THE KNOWLEDGE that Boom was okay and getting better, Asha felt comfortable enough to take a nap when she returned home. Before dozing off, she realized she didn't return his cellphone. That may have been a blessing in disguise. She couldn't call to check on him tonight, but in turn, he couldn't call to dissuade her from carrying out her mission.

She woke up at ten p.m. and dressed in all black. When considering the weaponry needed tonight, it was safe to assume Slim wouldn't be home alone. If she had to lay several people down, an assault rifle was ideal, but she preferred the mobility of the two pistols she toted earlier. She made sure to bring silencers for both guns and grabbed a ski mask before she left the house at 11.

Back in Slim's neighborhood, she found his home lively late into the night. In addition to the Escalade, there was another car parked in the driveway and two more in front of the house. It appeared every light inside the home was on. Asha did her due diligence and checked the back of the house while contemplating her plan of attack. In this neighborhood the alleyways were paved and free of debris. Slim's back fence was ten feet tall, made of wood. Without scaling it, she couldn't be certain that he didn't have dogs.

Back at the front of the house, she parked down the street and watched the happenings on Slim's property for nearly two hours. Even after one a.m., there was a steady stream of visitors, mostly females. Some remained inside the house, while others left after an hour or so. Each time the door opened, the guests were greeted by the smiling face of one of Slim's henchmen. Asha could tell there was a party atmosphere inside. The men were indulging in liquor and women, possibly to celebrate Slim's rise to the top. Solomon had been defeated, and they bodied his hitman in the process. Asha fumed as she watched them. She couldn't wait to rain on their parade.

By two a.m., she believed she'd gathered enough intel to move forward. The activity at Slim's house had slowed by then. From her vantage point, Asha had determined there were at least six people inside the house, three of whom were female. One of her targets was a man in a red shirt who she suspected was inebriated. Each time he came to the door, he toted a bottle of D'Ussé that had been gradually drained as the night wore on. Asha had seen him turn the bottle up and take a manly swig when he opened the door earlier that night. She hoped the rest of the bottle had gone down the same way.

Her next target had only answered the door once. He wore a white tee and was the more burly of the two. The main target was Slim, but Asha hadn't laid eyes on him all night. There was a chance he wasn't home, but her intuition told her he was. The Escalade he was riding in earlier that day was parked out front. She doubted if he'd take a pass on whatever freaky situation they had going on in his place.

Her heart drummed with the beat of war as she screwed the silencers onto her pistols. She placed both guns in her double holster and checked the duffle bag on the passenger seat. Inside the bag, she had all the equipment Boom would've brought with him. The only thing missing was the brawn needed to kick in the front door, but there were other ways to gain entry.

Asha checked the house again and realized she might not have to work as hard as she thought. The door opened again, and she saw that one of the women was leaving. The man with the red shirt stood chatting with her in the doorway before closing it. The woman wore high heels and a short skirt. If Asha had to guess, she'd label her a high-priced whore. But maybe that wasn't the case. Maybe she just liked to dress like one.

What was clear was the woman was having trouble pulling gravity, her heels and whatever drugs or alcohol she had in her system, together to perform the simple task of walking to her car. The man with the red shirt was no gentleman. He did not linger long enough to see if she made it down the sidewalk. Asha quickly altered her plans and left her car with both pistols in hand. She crept through the night quickly and quietly. If the drunk woman had her wits about her, she would've seen her coming. Instead, she made it to her car and had her back to the demon when Asha announced herself.

"Don't say shit," she hissed. *"Get down! Duck yo head down!"* With a strong hand on her shoulder, she forced her in the direction she wanted her to go. *"Get down, bitch!"*

The woman couldn't stop a surprised yelp from escaping her. Asha slammed the butt of her gun into the back of her head to shut her up.

"*Ho, I said be quiet! Get down! Get yo ass down!*"

"*Please! Please stop!*"

"*Shut up!*"

The woman was frazzled but compliant. She dropped to her knees next to her car. Asha shoved her down further, until she was face down on the pavement. She crouched next to her and planted a knee on her back. She buried the barrel of her pistol in her hair.

"You feel that?" she whispered. "You know what that is, don't you?"

"*Please*," the woman cried, whispering now. "*Please don't do this.*"

"*I asked you if you know what this is!*" Asha hissed.

"*A gun! You got a gun!*"

"That's right, ho." From her crouched position, Asha checked the front of the house. There was no movement. The door remained closed. "You wanna die tonight?" she asked.

"*No. Please, don't do it. I don't wanna die.*"

"What's your name?"

"Wha, what?"

"Bitch, what's your name?"

"*Brisha*! Oh my God. I peed on myself."

Asha ignored that gross bit of news. At this point in her career, she'd encountered pissy pants so many times it was almost par for the course.

"Listen, Brisha, I'm gonna give you the chance to make it home tonight, but you gotta do exactly what I tell you. You cool with that?"

"Yes, please don't kill me. *Please.*"

"The first thing you gotta do is *not scream*," Asha told her. "No matter what happen when I help you up, and no matter what happen when we get in that house, rule number one is *don't scream.* If you scream, I ain't got no use for you, and you gon' be the first one I kill. You got that?"

"*Oh, my God, please don't kill me.*"

"Brisha, I'm starting to think you not gon' be no help to me. If you can't get past rule number one, I might as well kill yo ass right now."

"*No, please! I won't scream. I promise, I won't scream.*"

"You sure, Brisha?"

"I'm sure. I promise I won't."

"Alright, Brisha. I'ma trust you. You bet not let me down..."

CHAPTER 38

THE MAN WITH the red shirt did not think anything was amiss when he answered the door and saw Brisha standing there. He grinned.

"Damn, bitch. You want some more of this dick?"

At that point, Brisha only had one line – *Can I use the bathroom right quick* – but she couldn't get it out. Asha stood off to the side of the door, concealed by the darkness and the bushes. Only the whites of her eyes shone as she watched the maybe-hooker stumble over her words.

"Can I, cuh, I can…"

To make matters worse, Brisha panicked and looked to Asha for guidance. At that point, the gig was up, but it didn't matter. Asha sprang from the shadows like a nightmare. Before the man could react, she shoved Brisha into him. The drunk girl stumbled forward and rolled into his feet. The man with the red shirt maintained his footing but not the better part of his brain. Asha sent him flying with two to the head.

THUMP! THUMP!

The silenced pistols were not completely silent, but they made less sound than the man did as he fell to the floor in a twisted heap.

A quick scan of the front room revealed it was empty. Asha kicked the door closed and moved to the kitchen with both guns raised. The man with the white shirt stood at the counter. Alerted by the commotion in the living room, he looked up from a plate of chicken wings. Both hands greasy, he neither had time to drop the wing he'd been gnawing on or reach for a weapon before he caught two to the chest.

THUMP! THUMP!

Asha hurried around the corner and finished him off with one to the head.

THUMP!

Back in the front room, Brisha was still on the floor, balled up like an elementary student during a tornado drill. Asha approached her but kept her eyes trained on the hallway ahead of them.

"Get up."

"*Oh my God, oh my God, oh my God...*"

"Brisha, you fucking up," Asha warned her. Adrenaline made the blood course through her veins hot and hard. The hairs stood on her arms. Behind the ski mask, her eyes were dilated, her mouth set in a sneer.

"*I didn't scream,*" Brisha cried. "*I didn't scream.*"

"*Get up!*"

She kicked the woman in the shoulder and couldn't fault Brisha for yelping like a scared puppy.

"Bitch, if you don't get yo ass up."

Brisha made it to her feet, and Asha shoved her forward, down the hallway. The pistol she'd used still had plenty bullets, but she stuffed it into her holster and swapped the unused gun to her dominant hand. With her free hand, she grabbed a handful of the hair on the back of Brisha's head and held her at arm's length, guiding her in the direction she wanted her to go. She heard music coming from somewhere upstairs, but she couldn't head in that direction until she cleared every room on the first floor.

Brisha was stiff at first, wobbling on legs that couldn't quite find their rhythm, but after the first two rooms, she understood her role. She was the masked woman's human shield. The only thing she could do about it was follow the puppeteer's instructions precisely, so she wouldn't get her brains blown out. She prayed that whoever was inside the rooms didn't start shooting first.

At each stop, Asha was quick and methodical. If the door was closed, she ordered Brisha to, *"Open it."* If the door was already open, she marched in with her crash test dummy. Either way, they were in and out in less than five seconds.

When they finished checking downstairs, Asha encountered resistance when she led her hostage to the stairs. Brisha wasn't unwilling to climb them, but by then she had almost reached the point where she *couldn't.* The stress combined with the intoxicants she'd consumed had taken its toll. She fell to her knees at the foot of the stairs and sobbed uncontrollably.

"Brisha, get the fuck up!" Asha whispered. "We almost done."

The woman squeezed her eyes closed, shaking her head from side to side. *"I can't. I can't go no more. Please don't kill me."*

Asha debated leaving her behind. With the first two men dead, she was all but certain Slim was the last man standing. But he might have sensed something was wrong and fortified his position. If Asha was headed for a shootout, she'd be damned if Brisha didn't eat the first bullet.

She delivered a kick to her ass and then slammed her face against the second stair. The stairway was carpeted, but the force was hard enough to open a gash on the bridge of her nose. Before she could cry out in pain, Asha shoved her pistol hard into her cheek.

"*Make one sound, and it's gon' be the last one you make,*" she growled. "*Now get yo fonky ass up.*"

She yanked the woman up by her hair and had second thoughts about attacking her. It probably wasn't a good idea if Brisha saw stars in addition to whatever problems she was already having walking, but the sudden violence did the trick. Brisha made it to her feet and marched up the stairs like a soldier. When they reached the top, Asha tracked the music to the door straight ahead of them. The other rooms were probably empty, but she made sure to clear them first.

When they reached the last one, both she and Brisha knew this was the end of the road. Asha readied herself and steadied her position. "Alright," she said, "when I say go, open it fast. Push it all the way open. You ready?"

"*Yes. Ple, please don't shoot me.*"

"*Alright, go!*" Asha whispered. "*Open it!*"

Brisha pushed the door open, and Asha shoved her inside, the same way she'd done half a dozen times already. The only difference now was this room was occupied by three people. Over Brisha shoulder, Asha saw that they were all on the bed, all of them naked. Slim was balls deep in one girl, plowing her from the back. The other girl lie on her back with her legs spread wide, getting ate out by the one Slim was fucking. A Trey Songz tune filled the room. Asha shoved Brisha onto the bed and drew her other pistol. She was the only person in the room armed. All eyes were on her.

"*Don't nobody move!*" she barked.

Slim was the only one itching to do so. The shock in his eyes had already transitioned to outrage.

Asha told him, "Unless you gon' shoot me with yo dick, you know you can't do shit about what's about to go down. Better, be easy, nigga. Brisha, get yo ass over here."

The woman rolled off the bed and looked up at her with her eyes and nose leaking. "*Please. Please don't kill me.*"

Asha sneered at her. "Damn. You gots to be the most crying motherfucker I ever seen! Get on yo knees and crawl over here." When the woman complied, Asha instructed her to, "Reach in my front pocket and grab these zip ties..."

Brisha was so compliant by then, Asha didn't have to train either gun on her as she did what she was told. Instead, her attention was focused on the man of the house.

"Slim, put yo hands behind yo back. Keep yo dick in that bitch."

Slim registered surprise that she knew his name. He didn't move.

Only Asha knew that he was going to die anyway. She told him, "I'm just here to rob you. I know you don't like what's going on, but if you play it cool, you'll make it through this. You can make the money back. A month from now, it'll be like this never happened. But we can go the other route, if you want to. Brisha, tell him what happened to them niggas downstairs."

"*They, they dead,*" she bawled. "*They both dead.*"

That news further infuriated Slim, but he was smart enough to know there was a difference between a robbery and a homicide. He moved his hands behind his back, and Brisha went to secure them. Asha moved in that direction too, to make sure she did it right.

"Tighter," she said.

"Okay, okay. Please. I'm doing it. I'm doing it."

With Slim bound, Asha was able to let her guard down a little. She made Brisha bind the other two girls, and then she put her gun down and used her last zip tie for Brisha. They were listening to a Drake song by then. No one said a word. With all four hostages sitting on the bed, three of them nude, Asha took a moment to admire her handiwork. Even though Boom didn't want her to pursue this, she knew he'd be proud of what she'd singlehandedly accomplished.

She then told Slim, "Alright, nigga. Get up. Come show me where the money at."

Slim reluctantly rose to his feet. Before they left the room, she debated whether she should kill the three women. She decided against it. Boom had taught her to avoid harming innocents whenever possible.

"Brisha," she said, "tell these ho's what'll happen if they try something slick before we get back."

"She gon' kill us," the girl cried. *"Please, y'all, don't do nothing. She'll kill us all."*

The naked girls looked sufficiently shook, so Asha left it at that. "Come on, nigga," she told Slim. "I ain't got all night."

CHAPTER 39

SLIM WAS COOPERATIVE throughout most of the ordeal. Before they left the bedroom, he begged Asha to let him put his pants on, but she refused. With his arms bound behind him, he led her downstairs to where he said his safe was in the master bedroom. When he saw her handiwork on the living room floor, he was even more agreeable. He led her into the closet of the room in question and told her where the safe was hidden behind a row of neatly hung dress shirts. He gave her the combination, and Asha opened it with her gloved hands. Her mouth watered when she estimated nearly half a million in cash inside, along with a few Rolexes and expensive rings.

But she didn't immediately go for the money. She turned back to Slim, her gun pointed at his chest, and told him to go back to the bedroom. He began to shake his head.

"Wha, what's wrong?"

"Nothing," she said. "Go sit on the bed."

"I don't, I don't want to." He swallowed roughly. "What's wrong?"

Asha's goal was to avoid having to step over his body and through his blood on the way out. But if he chose to inconvenience her with this last act of defiance, she was okay with it.

She asked him, "Why you kill Solomon?"

His eyes grew large. He blinked several times before shaking his head. "I – I didn't. I didn't kill him."

"You paid to have it done."

"No, no..." His frown was so extreme, it aged him right before her eyes. "I didn't do that. *I didn't have nothing to do with that.*"

"But you fucking his woman. And you knew he put a hit out on you. You had every reason to go after him. It woulda been stupid if you didn't."

Slim's eyes filled with tears – real tears. They rolled down his cheeks on both sides. "*Please don't kill me. I gave you everything I have.* I didn't have nothing to do with Solomon getting killed. I swear to God I didn't."

Asha watched him for a few seconds. She was being honest when she said, "You know what, Slim, I believe you. The only problem is you'll probably come after Boom sooner or later, when you find out he alive."

"Wait, you – what?"

THUMP!

She sat him down with one to the chest. She stood over him and put two more in his head.

THUMP! THUMP!

The room was suddenly silent, other than her breaths. She never felt great about murdering a man, but as she looked down at the mess she'd made of Slim's face, a dark, sick feeling enveloped her. This was not the man who shot Boom. He had not wronged them in any way. If she hadn't killed him for revenge, what was it for? She wanted to believe it was because he was a potential witness. Slim knew she was a woman, and even if he didn't say it, he had to know she was Brionna. He would've come after her and Boom sooner or later, wouldn't he?

She looked back at the safe, not wanting to believe the root of all evil had ensnared her in its dark, grisly grip. Her heart began to thump loudly, pumping what felt like venom throughout her body. She shook it off and turned her back on him.

She felt no joy in emptying the contents of the safe into a suitcase. But like a moth drawn to a flame, she felt compelled, almost obligated to do so.

Back upstairs, she found the naked women conniving, attempting to make a phone call. One had managed to get hold of a cellphone. With her arms behind her, she tried to manipulate the device, while her friend watched her hands and guided her. They both froze when Asha appeared in the doorway. Brisha sat on the other end of the bed crying.

"I told 'em not to," she muttered. "I told 'em. I told 'em not to..."

Asha raised her weapon. The naked women cried and huddled together, wanting so desperately to hold each other, but they couldn't.

Asha hardened her heart.

These women were not innocents. They were witnesses. Even with a ski mask on, they would be able to identify the suspect of these cold-blooded murders as a female. The police might not be able to track Asha down based solely on that, but the streets would know who had done this. *Brionna* would be on the lips of every gangster within 24 hours.

Asha's arm began to tremble. She took a shuddering breath and lowered her weapon. She looked around the room and spotted a purse on the floor. There was another on the dresser.

"Them y'all purses?" she asked.

The girls couldn't find their voices. Their eyes were as big as half dollars. One of them nodded.

Asha raided the purses until she found both of their ID's.

"*Courtney Washington*," she said, "and *Alycia Horn*. When the police get here, I need to know what y'all gon' tell 'em. 'Cause if I gotta worry about y'all saying it was a female who did this, I'd be better off leaving no witnesses."

"*No, no*," the one named Courtney said. "I ain't gon' say shit! I don't know nothing."

"You gotta know *something*," Asha said. "Somebody had to tie you up..."

"It was a man," Alycia said.

"*A big, black man*," Courtney added. "He had a mask on."

"Y'all sure about that?" Asha asked. "'Cause I'ma keep these ID's, and I ain't got no problem going to these addresses and killing whoever there."

"*We sure!*" Courtney promised. "*We ain't got shit to do with this!*"

"What about you, Brisha?" Asha asked.

Brisha was so busted up and traumatized, her voice was soft and robotic. She didn't look Asha's way. Her reply was without emotion, but it was the correct response. "A big, black man, wearing a mask."

"Alright," Asha said, lowering her weapon. "I hope this the last time I see any of y'all, but if I hear anything different than what y'all saying now, trust me, it won't be."

She backed out of the room and quickly made her way down the stairs.

A minute later, she was back in her car.

Ten minutes after that, she had made it to the freeway.

CHAPTER 40

ASHA WAS NOT a heavy drinker, but Boom had a well-stocked bar at home. She approached it in the darkness of the den, not wanting to turn on the lights and expose herself, not even to herself. She selected a bottle of Jameson whiskey and cringed at the thought of the taste before even trying it. She hefted a bottle of red berry Ciroc instead. Standing in the darkness, she twisted off the cap and took a manly swig, much like the man in the red shirt had done earlier tonight. The liquor was more harsh than sweet, but it was acceptable.

She took the bottle to the bedroom and took another long drink. And then another as she got into the shower. She wasn't nearly as bloody as she was the night Boom was shot, but no matter how long she washed herself, she couldn't scrub away her sins. She had done many horrible things since joining Boom's team. But even despicable acts, like shooting BD in the dick, didn't compare to what had happened at Slim's house.

Tonight, she felt as if she'd crossed the line. She couldn't blink without seeing Brisha's face, stricken with fear and agony. She couldn't get the woman's wails out of her head.

I can't. I can't go no more. Please don't kill me.

She gon' kill us. Please, y'all, don't do nothing. She'll kill us all.

And Slim – he was by no means innocent. He was a drug dealer, a hoodlum – by any definition a menace to society. But Asha had not been paid to murder him, and she had achieved no vengeance by doing so. The only thing she had gained was a suitcase full of dirty money and a conscious that would not lot her escape the fact there were levels of evil and she had propelled herself to the furthest spectrum.

The bottle of Ciroc did not alleviate her guilt, but when she drained it, the liquor did help her fall back into bed and accept what she had become. The truth was everything she did was for Boom. It had been this way since the first day she met him. In a biblical sense, she understood that Boom deserved to lose his life for the sins he'd committed. They both did. But until the day came when she breathed her last breath, she would annihilate anyone who even *thought* about hurting her soulmate. She would harm an innocent to acquire the funds needed for their retirement.

At this point, no one could stop her – not even the man she was doing it for.

CHAPTER 41

THE NEXT MORNING, she awakened to a blaring headache and a call from a number she recognized but had not memorized. She checked the display on the phone and saw that it was not morning after all. It was one o'clock in the afternoon. She tried to shake the fog from her head as she answered the call.

"Hello."

"Hi." She recognized the voice. It was Doc. "Do you have access to a van?" he asked. "I need you to come get your boyfriend today."

Asha sat up, frowning. "Come get him? What you mean?"

"He's well enough to go home," the vet said. "He's not 100 percent. He should remain on bed rest for a couple more days. Even then, he'll require therapy before he's moving around like he used to. But he's well enough to leave my hospital."

Asha shook her head. She was rewarded with a dull pain behind her eyes. "If he can't get out of bed, why you making him leave?"

"Because I'm not set up to do this long term. Every day he's here is another day someone could find out about him. If that happens, I would lose everything – not to mention all the questions the police will have for Boom. He's still on a few drips. I'll show you how to change them out and what you'll need to do to make sure his bandages are changed, and his wounds are clean. He may need help going to the bathroom."

Asha couldn't believe what she was hearing. "You putting him out, and he can't go to the bathroom on his own?"

"He can go," Doc said, "but he needs assistance. I've been helping him up and getting him to a walker. But he managed to do it by himself last night. There's nothing he needs at this point that you can't do. Do you have a van? I need you to come get him today, after closing time. I'll let you keep the lift table. I should be able to lower it enough to fit in a van. Don't worry. If you have any problems when you get him home, you can call me, and I'll walk you through it."

Asha was eager to have her man home, but she didn't like the timing. Before meeting Boom, she worked in construction. The thought of being responsible for medical care at this level freaked her out. Plus, she knew Boom would give her a hard time about completing her mission. She had at least one more murder on her to-do list. It was easier to be a renegade when Boom wasn't around.

"Yeah, I have a van," she said, thinking of the Savana Boom had used when he enlisted OG Cali and his crew to help rob Pacman's dealers. "What time you want me to be there?"

CHAPTER 42

SHE HAD A few hours to kill before heading to Cedar Hill to pick up her man, so Asha went to meet with her cousin again. Tristan seemed apprehensive when he came down the stairs of his apartment and sat in the car next to her. Once again, he was taken aback by her appearance. Today she wore a tank top with tight jeans and sneakers. Her eyes were hidden behind large, designer shades. Her frizzy mane was concealed by a wig. The hair was long and straight, flowing past her shoulders. She had a nose ring and a spattering of freckles on both cheeks.

Tristan shook his head, staring at her. "So, them wasn't real tattoos you had the other day?"

Asha shook her head.

"Why you ain't tell me?" he asked. "I asked what was up with them. You coulda said it was some kind of disguise..."

Asha looked around the parking lot, always wary of her surroundings. She told him, "Tristan, I love you. But it's gon' be some things about me that I can't talk about. If you start asking the wrong kind of questions, I'm either gon' lie to you or not answer at all. Sorry it gotta be that way. But it is what it is."

He frowned. She didn't care if he accepted it.

"What's going on in the hood?" she asked him. "You heard anything?"

He held his hard gaze, and then his features softened. "Yeah. Slim and some of his niggas got killed last night."

Asha didn't react to the news.

"It was some ho's there," Slim continued. "They talking 'bout it was some big, black dude that did it. People wondering if it was Boom. They say the way that shit went down, ain't nobody coulda pulled it off *but* Boom. They wondering if that nigga really dead..."

Asha didn't say anything.

Tristan sighed. "You could at least tell me if he alive or not. 'Cause if it wasn't him, I was thinking it had to be you. But them bitches said it was a dude..."

When she still didn't respond, he said, "Come on, Asha. This ain't cool. You want me to tell you everything I know, but you won't tell me nothing. You actin' like you don't trust a nigga."

"It ain't that I don't trust you, Tristan. I just can't have you in my business like that. You not my partner in crime. You my family. Those are two different lanes."

"Yeah, I know. And you want me to stay in my lane."

"That's the best thing for you – and your family."

"But you want me to be your informant."

"If that's what you wanna call it. There's one more person I need to holler at..."

"Who, Lynx?"

"Yeah. How you know?"

"That's the last nigga on Solomon's hit list."

"You know where he at?"

"I know where one of his spots is," he admitted. "But you don't think I should feel some kind of way about the people I'm telling you about ending up dead?"

"Some kind of way like what? Like you responsible? Trust me, they gon' end up dead whether you help me or not."

"I know, but damn, cuz... This shit, I ain't never been involved in nothing like this."

There was nothing Asha could say to make him feel better about that. All she could offer was, "It'll be over soon."

"You know Lynx is prolly on high alert," he said, "especially after what happened to Slim. If I knew Boom was alive, I'd feel way better about telling you where Lynx is. But if you going after him by yourself, that ain't a smart move. If something happen to you, I'ma feel like it's my fault."

"We choose our own paths, Tristan. I don't need you to worry about me or feel bad if something happen to me. I know what I'm doing."

Her cousin was doubtful about that, but he didn't deny her the information she requested.

CHAPTER 43

THREE HOURS LATER, Asha parked on a quiet street in an east side neighborhood that had more vacant houses than occupied ones. Ahead of her, three houses down, in a duplex on the corner, she saw a cherry red Camaro slow to a stop alongside the curb. She'd been waiting for over two hours for Lynx's flashy ride to make an appearance. The duplex wasn't his home, but according to Tristan, it was his newest dope spot. Lynx had one of his cousins working it for him.

Two men emerged from the Camaro. Tristan's description of Lynx was spot on, as well as his assertion that Lynx never let anyone drive his car. Asha's next target was of medium height with a stocky build. He was bald with fair skin and no facial hair. The moment Asha laid eyes on him, she knew he was not the man who shot Solomon and Boom. Once again, she wasn't sure how she knew, but it was not something she was on the fence about. She was positive this wasn't the shooter.

She frowned, trying to make sense of her intuition, but it did not make sense.

Unfortunately for Lynx, whether he was the man who actually pulled the trigger or not didn't matter. He may still be responsible. The only way to rule him out was to question him directly. Asha was confident that if she looked him in the eyes and demanded the truth, she would know if he was being honest with her. She was also confident that Lynx would not live to tell the story, if she got the opportunity to question him.

The dealer was inside the duplex for ten minutes. When he left, Asha followed him to a house in the Stop Six neighborhood. She wasn't sure if this was where he lay his head at night, but she had two locations to start with when she resumed her hunt after dark.

CHAPTER 44

SHE HEADED FOR one of their safe houses and swapped vehicles before driving to Doc's animal hospital. When she got there, she found the side gate open. She pulled behind the main building and parked in front of the large animal surgery unit. She knocked on the door. Doc came and opened it a moment later. He stepped outside and checked out her van.

He told her, "Yeah, this should do. Lemme see the keys, so I can back it in for you."

Asha tossed him the keys and went inside to check on Boom. The vet had moved him to the front of the building, to the area where he had operated on him. Boom lie on the same lift table he'd been on for the past two days. His blanket was tucked tightly around his body. He was connected to an IV line, but the bags of medicine lie on his chest, rather than hang from an IV pole. He was ready for transport.

Asha approached the table and placed a hand on his shoulder. Boom's eyes were closed, his breathing steady. He looked very peaceful.

"Hey, baby," she said. "You ready to go home?"

He didn't respond.

Asha moved her hand to his cheek and stroked it tenderly. "Wake up, sleepy head."

Still no response.

She moved her hand back to his shoulder and shook him slightly. "Baby. Hey. Enzo...?"

When he still didn't respond, she frowned.

She might have stood there trying to rouse him for an hour, but Doc returned and told her, "Oh, don't bother trying to wake him up. In preparation for his trip, I gave him enough meds to keep him comfortable for the next couple of hours."

"Comfortable," Asha asked, "or knocked out?"

"I guess *knocked out* would be another way to describe it," Doc conceded. "He's gonna get jostled a little bit while we're moving the table. If he was awake, it wouldn't feel good at all."

When they wheeled the table outside, Asha saw that the vet had provided a ramp to help roll it into the van. Even still, it took both of them to push the table up the incline. Asha knew it would be easier going down, but she worried about how she'd manage on her own when she got home. If Doc had the same concerns, he didn't mention it. Asha felt like he was so eager to get Boom out of his building, he could care less what happened when they hit the road.

The vet climbed inside the van and strapped the table to the front seats. He returned to the building and came back with a walker. He put it in the van, next to the table.

"Oh, one more thing…"

He went into the building again. This time he brought an IV pole. He collapsed it and put it in the van. Asha's feeling of unease grew by the second.

He closed the back doors, and told her, "Boom said he'll send you to pay the remainder of his balance tomorrow. Could you call before you come? Since you already showed your face here, it would be best if I met you outside."

Asha's nostrils flared, but she didn't say what was on her mind. She simply told him, "Alright."

Before she took off, the vet gave her last minute instructions, ending with, "You can call me, if you forget any of this. But I'm sure it'll be fine. Boom's strong. He's already recovering a lot faster than I expected."

Asha agreed that her man was strong, but getting discharged less than 48 hours after being shot twice, with one bullet traveling deep in his back, didn't seem right at all. She got behind the wheel and cringed every time she encountered a bump on the way out of the parking lot. She was afraid to hit the speed limit on the road and the freeway.

By the time she made it home, she was a bundle of nerves.

CHAPTER 45

GETTING THE LIFT bed out of the van, into their home and all the way to the den proved to be as difficult as she envisioned, but she managed. Asha was drenched with sweat by the time she finished setting up the IV pole and hanging the bags. True to his word, the meds the vet gave Boom kept him comfortable and asleep the whole time. Asha was a little irritated by that. A part of her wished Boom was awake, so he would know how hard she'd worked for him.

The sun had set by then, so she showered and got dressed for the night. Once again, she opted for all black. She planned to don her ski mask, so she didn't bother with a wig or makeup to alter her appearance. She left the closet and returned to the den to check on Boom. She found him awake but still drowsy. He looked her way and then at his surroundings.

"How, how you get me in here?" he asked, his voice as weak as he looked.

She stepped to the lift table and kissed him softly. "It wasn't easy, but I managed."

"You did it all by yourself?"

"*Uh, yeah.* I didn't wanna ask the neighbors to help get my shot-up boyfriend in the house."

If Boom found that amusing, it didn't show.

"You hungry?" she asked. "Doc said you haven't eaten since twelve, and you didn't eat much then."

He nodded. "Yeah, I guess I can eat. What'd you cook?"

"Nothing yet. You got something in mind?"

"Can you make some pancakes and sausage. Been craving your pancakes."

"You want breakfast for dinner?"

"I been sleep so much, I don't know when the sun's coming or going."

"You still want the pancakes?"

"Yeah. I can try to straighten out my days and nights tomorrow."

"Okay."

It only took twenty minutes to prepare the meal. By then, Boom had mostly overcome the sedatives the vet gave him. By the time he was done eating, he was fully awake. While he consumed the pancakes, Asha told him what happened last night with Slim and his crew. Boom didn't look upset with her when she was done talking.

But he did tell her, "You doing the most."

She stood next to his table watching him. She took his plate and utensils and placed them on the coffee table.

She told him, "This is coming from the man who blew up Mr. Brown's house with a grenade launcher."

"I did that to find out where you was," Boom replied. "Yo life was in danger."

"And you got shot. I had to ride on them niggas for that."

"Even if it wasn't the ones who shot me...?"

She shrugged. "Yeah. Why not? The streets need to know what happens if they fuck with us."

Boom stared at her, as if seeing her for the first time.

"Lynx didn't shoot you either," she informed him. "But tonight, I'ma find out if he had anything to do with it. Either way, that nigga dead."

Boom frowned. "What you mean? How you know he didn't shoot me?"

"I saw him today. It ain't him."

His frown intensified. "You keep saying these ain't the people who shot me. But you also said you didn't see who did it. Why you so sure it wasn't Slim or Lynx?"

"I don't know. I been trying to figure that out myself."

Boom wanted to follow her line of thinking until they got to the bottom of it, but there was something else he wanted more. He told her, "Stay home. We'll handle the rest of this when I get better."

She shook her head. "No, I'm handling this tonight. You stay here and rest. I'll be back in a little bit."

She took his plate to the kitchen. When she returned, Boom was trying to sit up on his elbows. She could see how the attempt pained him. She stepped to him to push him back to a lying position, but she feared he'd grab her arm and keep holding it until she changed her mind about leaving. She stopped a safe distance away. He stared at her with what could be described as resentment in his eyes.

"Girl, is you listening to me? I'm telling you to stay home."

"Enzo, I done already told you I'm leaving. You taught me to do this. It's a little too late to decide you don't like it."

"I taught you to kill for a reason."

"You taught me to kill for *money*. The way I see it, it don't make a difference if it's a hit or if I kill somebody and *take* they money. Either way, I'm getting the money. We done killed plenty people who never did us no harm. Why you got a problem with it now?"

He gave up his fight with gravity and fell back onto the table. He had to catch his breath before he told her, "I ain't got a problem with you killing somebody. I got a problem with you doing it by yourself."

"You gotta trust that you trained me right. If you did, I shouldn't have no problem taking care of the last person on my list. I told you what I did last night. I took control of a house with six people in it *by myself.*"

Frustrated, Boom tried another line of reasoning. "What's supposed to happen to me if you don't come home? I can barely get out this bed to take a piss. What if I need some help?"

Asha knew that was coming. She pulled his cellphone from her pocket and tossed it onto his legs. "You can call me if it's an emergency. Or you can call Doc. He said he'll help if we need him."

"*That nigga way the fuck in Cedar Hill.*"

"If you offer him enough money, he'll come. He'll break the door down to get in here, as long as he's getting paid. You know that as well as I do."

He shook his head in exasperation. "I can't believe this shit."

"I can't believe you don't trust me to take care of this. I love you, Enzo. I'm doing this for you – for both of us." She stared into his eyes as she backed out of the room. "Try to get some rest, baby. I shouldn't be long…"

When she made it to the kitchen and could no longer see him, his hold over her was not as powerful.

"Asha!"

She shook her head and grabbed her duffle bag off the counter before heading to the garage.

218

PART SIX
NON-BELIEVER

CHAPTER 46

AN HOUR LATER, she was in position. She wasn't sure if Lynx lived at the house she was watching, but this was the place she'd followed him to this afternoon, and his Camaro was still there. There was only one other car parked in the driveway. Asha surveyed the house from a distance. Contrary to Boom's argument, she wasn't taking her responsibility to care for him for granted. She was fully prepared for this mission and this stakeout. Killing Lynx was her primary objective, but making it home to her man took precedent.

To ensure she didn't get blindsided by anyone inside the home, Asha made sure to bring Boom's favorite binoculars. They were equipped with night vision and infrared technology. Sitting in her SUV, she studied the house carefully. Judging by the glowing, red figures, she knew there were two men inside, both in the front room. One appeared to be sitting, while the other had been moving around. From her vantage point, she wasn't sure what they were doing. As far as she could tell, they were both sitting ducks.

Her reconnaissance from the back of the house revealed a wire link fence, no dogs and a patio door made of glass. She knew how Boom would approach the situation, and she planned to do the same – toss flash and smoke grenades through the front, run around back while the targets were disoriented, breach the patio door and toss more flash bangs and smoke grenades through that entrance before entering. For optimal success, she would question Lynx about Boom's shooting and empty his safe before she silenced him.

With both eyes focused on the view from her binoculars, Asha was completely caught off guard by a light tap on her car window. Eyes wide, she slowly looked to the left. What she saw was so obscene, she scarcely believed it was real. She couldn't believe she'd allowed this to happen. But her eyes were not deceiving her. She was staring down the barrel of a pistol. The man holding it tapped on the window again with the steel barrel. This time he accompanied the tapping with instructions.

"Keep both yo hands on them binoculars. Keep 'em up, where I can see em."

With her windows rolled up, his voice was muffled, but Asha heard him clearly. She clenched her teeth.

Fuck.

Her duffle bag sat on the passenger seat. Both of her pistols were inside, along with the other equipment she'd brought along for this job. She glanced at the bag, and then her attention returned to the man standing next to her SUV. He was standing so close, she could only see the bottom half of his face, which had a short beard. His gun was black, less than two feet from her head. She knew she had no chance to reach for a gun, cock it and use it to defend herself.

Her mouth went dry. Her body heat raised the temperature in the cabin of the SUV. It didn't feel like her heart beat at all while she waited for her next instruction. The man wasn't uniformed, but she hoped he was a cop. Getting arrested was not ideal, but at least it wouldn't cost her her life.

She didn't see the man's hand move, but she heard him attempt to open her door. It was locked.

He told her, "Use your left hand to unlock this door. Keep holding them binoculars with your other hand. If you got a gun down there, you better think twice before you try to use it. Even if you shoot me through the door, you gon' hit me in the body. I'ma shoot you in the head before I go down."

Asha did not have a gun in the compartment under her door handle, but she wondered what would happen if she opened the door and shoved it into him in one hard motion. Would he get the shot off? She decided that even if he didn't – even if she managed to knock him down, which was unlikely – he'd recover before she had a chance to go for her gun.

Rather than *her* life flashing before her eyes, all she saw was Boom lying on his lift table in the den. He had taught her so much, but she could think of no training that addressed this scenario.

She pressed the button to unlock the door.

Upon hearing it, the man told her, "Alright. Now bring yo hand back up to them binoculars."

Asha sighed silently and followed his directions. He opened the door. The first thing she saw was his gun, a

Glock 19, pointed right at her. Beyond the gun, she saw that her assailant was tall, wearing all black, like herself. His expression was deadpan, as if shoving a gun in a woman's face was commonplace for him.

He gave her a onceover before saying, "You wanna tell me what the hell you doing?"

"Can I put my hands down?" she asked, looking up at him.

The man's eyes were without emotion. He told her, "Not yet. Why don't you answer my question first?"

She didn't bat an eye when she replied, "I'm with the neighborhood watch. Just doing my job, trying to keep the neighborhood safe."

"Oh yeah?" He grinned. "I'm with the neighborhood watch too. I guess we out here doing the same thing. Matter of fact, we having a neighborhood watch meeting *right now*. You should come."

She shook her head. "Nah, I'm good."

"Oh, shit. That's my bad. Sometimes I be saying shit like it's a question when it ain't. What I meant to say was get yo ass out the car. I get it right that time?"

"You ain't got no right to treat me like this."

"You might be right. You might be neighborhood watch. Hell, you might be a goddamn *bird watcher*. But you know what I think?"

Asha didn't want to know.

He told her anyway. "I think you might be *Brionna*. Get yo ass out the car. If I have to say it again, a bullet come with it."

You know Lynx is prolly on high alert, especially after what happened to Slim.

Asha hadn't doubted her cousin when he told her that, but she didn't consider the possibility that Lynx was more conniving than she was. It was hard to accept that one of his men had gotten the drop on her. But until they put a bullet in her head, there was hope. She began plotting her plan for escape as she turned in her seat and moved one leg out of the car.

"Can I put these down?" she asked, referencing the binoculars, "so I can use my hands to get out."

The gunman said, "Yeah. Put 'em on the passenger seat with yo right hand. Put yo left hand on the steering wheel."

Asha placed one hand on the steering wheel and used the other to put the binoculars on her duffle bag. With her hand so close to her pistols, it was hard to restrain herself from trying to defend herself. But that would've been suicide.

"Alright," the man said. "Now come on."

He made her walk ahead of him, while he kept his gun trained on her back.

Asha continued to play innocent. "Where we going?"

"You know where we going. We going to that house you was watching. You gon' tell me you don't know who in there?"

"No. I don't know what's going on."

"Where yo guns at?" he asked.

"What guns?"

"The ones that go in that holster you wearing."

"They in the car."

"Ain't nobody ever told you you gotta stay strapped? You never know when some shit might pop off."

Asha fumed and didn't respond to that.

When they got to the house, the man knocked on the door. "*It's me, don't shoot*," he announced. "Got a little bird watcher with me."

A shorter man with a gold grill and pretty brown eyes answered. He looked from Asha to the man with the gun.

"Who this?"

"I'm betting this that bitch *Brionna*. Gone. Get in there."

He shoved her in the back. Brown Eyes stepped back as she stumbled inside.

"Yo, Lynx," Brown Eyes called over his shoulder. "Come check this shit out."

Lynx appeared from the hallway wearing a red tee with red track pants. He was a handsome man, well built. His red attire blended nicely with his brown skin. He eyed Asha and then his cohorts.

"Where this bitch come from?"

"Caught her outside watching yo place," the gunman said. "Bitch had binoculars and everything. She say she ain't Brionna, but I think this that bitch. You see she got them holsters. Bitch was finna do you." He closed the door behind them.

Lynx's eyes brightened as he stepped closer. "Oh, shit. *This is that bitch*! You was finna do me, ho?" He smiled. "T, this bitch was finna do me!"

The man with the brown eyes grinned. "Guess that mean you was finna do me too," he told Asha. "Ain't that how y'all get down? You gotta kill everybody in the house, don't you?"

Asha said, "I don't know what y'all talking about. I told him I was just watching the neighborhood."

"Oh, yeah," the gunman said. "She say she *neighborhood watch* – with some binoculars and two pistols. I guess she George Zimmerman."

"Naw, this that bitch," Lynx said, staring at her. "Brionna, where yo man at? Motherfuckers talking about Boom dead. I knew that nigga wasn't dead! What I tell you, T?"

Before T could respond, Lynx answered his own question.

"I said how a motherfucker dead if ain't no body? How the fuck you gon' say some nigga dead, and ain't nobody seen the body?"

"That's what you said," Brown Eyes, better known as T, agreed.

"What I wanna know is why you coming for me," Lynx said. "I know you and Boom is solid, as far as handling y'all business. But why y'all finishing off a dead man's hit list? Even if Solomon paid you up front, it don't make sense to keep killing people he wanted dead."

"They went after Slim 'cause he killed Solomon," T offered.

"That what it is?" Lynx asked her. "Y'all killed Slim to get revenge for him killing Solomon?"

Trapped inside a home with three men who meant her harm, Asha accepted the fact that this was probably the end of the line for her. If she was to meet her maker, she wanted closure first.

"We killed Slim because we *thought* he was the one who shot Solomon. But we found out it wasn't him. It was you. That's why I'm here."

Lynx looked genuinely surprised. "What you mean, it was me? Bitch, I didn't have shit to do with Solomon or yo nigga getting shot." He looked to his partners in crime. "Ay, she think *we* did that shit."

"I heard it was Slim," T said.

"Yup, that's what I heard too," the gunman behind her said.

Asha couldn't see the gunman's face, but she stared at Lynx and T and knew they weren't lying.

"Wait, so let me get this straight," Lynx said. "You brought yo ass over here to kill me 'cause you think I shot yo nigga..." He shook his head. "You was gon' do me for some shit I ain't do..." His smile returned. "Bet you feeling stupid right about now."

"Actually," she said, "I feel a lot better. If you didn't shoot Boom, then I ain't got no beef with you. If you let me go, I'll tell 'em you straight, and he won't come looking for you. He knows where I am. If I don't make it home, he'll come looking for me. Once he finds out what happened, you won't last a week out here. Even if you leave the state, he'll find you. You know he will."

Lynx's smile faltered.

The man with the gun said, "Fuck that shit. I'm finna kill this bitch."

Asha continued to watch Lynx's eyes, hoping her hard, confident stare would bolster her threat. When his eyes moved away from her, she thought he was looking at the man standing behind her.

But he said, "Nigga, you lock the door?"

A second later, Asha heard someone burst through the opening. And then she heard voices.

"*Nigga, drop that shit!*"

"*Get down, nigga! Down!*"

"*Get yo bitch ass down!*"

For half a second, Asha thought Boom had come to her rescue. But she recognized one of the voices, even before she turned to see who it was. It was her cousin. She looked back and saw Tristan standing in the doorway with a pistol pointed at the gunman's back. An unknown man accompanied him. He kept Lynx and T at bay with another gun.

Asha had a dozen questions about how and why this was happening, but they could wait. She crouched and drew a Baretta from her ankle holster in one smooth motion. She charged Lynx, pointing the gun at his face.

"*Don't move*," she growled.

She made her way around him, so she could survey the whole scene. She was surprised to see that Tristan had not unarmed the man with the beard.

"*Drop that shit*!" she barked. "*Get on yo knees! Both of y'all!*"

The bearded man reluctantly dropped his weapon. He and T slowly dropped to their knees.

Asha pressed the barrel of her gun against the back of Lynx's neck. "Where the money?" she demanded.

"Don't give it to her," the bearded man said. "They gon' kill us anyway."

"I'm sick of yo ass," Asha said. "*Kill that nigga*," she instructed Tristan.

He hesitated.

Asha's frown was gruesome as she stomped towards them. Without a word, she raised her gun to the bearded man's melon and shot him herself.

PAP!

Tristan and his friend watched in disbelief.

Asha marched back to Lynx and returned to her position behind him. She repeated her request. *"Where the money?"*

"Just kill me," he said. "You ain't finna do me like y'all did Slim – take my money and my life. Fuck y'all."

"I told you why I killed that nigga Slim. You say you ain't had shit to do with Boom getting shot, and I believe you. If you don't give it up, I ain't just gon' kill you. I'ma do you like I did BD. You wanna know how long that nigga was on the ground squirming, holding the little piece of dick he had left, before I showed him mercy and put one in his head?"

Lynx did not want to know. *"Fuck it."* His breaths came hot and hard. "It's in the bedroom. Take it and leave me the fuck alone."

"Alright. Show me."

She followed him down the hall to one of the bedrooms.

Lynx pointed to the bottom drawer of his dresser and said, "It's in there."

She told him, "You get it."

She kept her gun on him as he yanked the drawer open. All she saw was clothes at first. He tossed them aside, and she saw nothing but cash.

"Grab one of those pillowcases," she instructed. "Put it in there."

Lynx took a pillow from his bed and shook the case free. He returned to the dresser and stuffed the money inside. *"Here!"*

She didn't take it from him.

"Naw, nigga. Where the dope. I want that too."

If fury was an expression, Lynx embodied it. But he wasn't foolish enough to say what was on his mind.

Through clenched teeth, he told her, "It's in the kitchen."

"Alright." She gestured with her pistol. "Come show me."

As they headed down the hallway, Asha was surprised to hear a loud **PAP!** in the living room, followed by shouting. Someone cried out in pain. The first gunshot was quickly followed by two more.

PAP!

PAP!

Walking ahead of her, Lynx had progressed far enough to see what was going on, while Asha's view was blocked by a wall. Whatever Lynx saw made his eyes widen. He looked back at her for a brief second before deciding he wanted in on the action in the front room. He turned in that direction. He only took two steps before Asha cut him down.

PAP!PAP!

Clutching his side, he fell to the ground groaning.

Asha rushed forward and was shocked by the scene before her. When she left Tristan and his friend, they were both armed. Lynx's last henchman, T, was on his knees without a weapon. Now Tristan's friend was on the floor, motionless. Tristan was on his back too, but he was still moving. He struggled with T over one of the guns. T stood over him, trying to wrestle it from his hands. If Asha didn't know any better, she'd swear they were fighting over the gun the bearded man had when he knocked on the window of her SUV.

How the fuck...?

Her look of bewilderment was replaced with anger. She raised her weapon and fired twice.

PAP!PAP!

She walked to the downed man and put another bullet in the side of his head.

PAP!

Looking down at her cousin, her confusion returned. *"What the hell happened?"*

Tristan panted as he tried to make it to his feet. *"Huh, I, I don't know, cuz. I thought my nigga was watching him."*

"Both of y'all was supposed to be watching him!"

As confounding as this was, she realized her anger was misguided. Tristan was no killer. He proved that when he didn't follow her instruction to kill the bearded man. Asha understood she was at fault for leaving her cousin in a room with an enemy who would do *anything* to save his life. She should've known better. She should've—

"Damn, cuz. I – I'm hit."

Tristan clutched his abdomen, unable to make it to his feet. Asha saw a bright blood stain blossoming on his tee shirt.

The wages of her sins hit her like a sledgehammer. *"Shit!"*

Before helping him up, she ran back to the hallway to check on Lynx. He appeared to be dying, but she couldn't risk it.

PAP!

A new hole above his left eye sealed the deal.

She snatched up the pillowcase and went back to her cousin. His friend had taken at least two shots, including one to the throat. There was no help for him.

"What you even doing here?" she asked as she grabbed all of the guns scattered on the floor, one by one. She threw them in the bag with the money before helping her cousin up.

"I, I came to help you," he managed. "I knew you was coming for this nigga. I saw 'em take you in here. I, I was, I was trying to... *Trying to, to help..."*

She got him to his feet, but he was fading fast. Tristan was not a large man, but Asha struggled to shoulder his weight as they staggered out of the door. When they reached the porch, she noticed her cousin wasn't wearing gloves. She dropped the pillowcase and took a second to wipe whatever prints might be on the doorknob. By then, Tristan was leaking badly. Asha bent to pick up the pillowcase and barely had enough strength to get them back to a standing position.

Somehow, they made it to her SUV down the street.

CHAPTER 47

AN HOUR LATER, Tristan was barely conscious in the passenger seat. Asha slammed on the brakes and threw the SUV in park. She hopped out of the truck and ran to the passenger side.

"*Please*," she cried, tears streaming down her face. "*Please help!*"

Doc looked angrier than a mama possum protecting her brood. He was just as angry when she called him on the way to the animal hospital. But at least he showed up. He approached the passenger window to assess his patient. He saw that Tristan was breathing and moaning.

He shook his head and blew out a sigh. "Follow me around back, and I'll see what I can do."

CHAPTER 48

WHEN SHE MADE it home, Boom could've said I told you so. He could've said she didn't accomplish anything tonight, and it was effectively her fault that Tristan got shot. But he didn't. He listened to her and then stroked her back and shoulders when she leaned over the lift table and rested her head on his chest. He told her to go bathe and to put everything she had on in a garbage bag, so they could dispose of it later.

When she got out of the shower, Asha ran a bath for her man. She could see how much it pained him to walk, but he was grateful to be on his feet. With his walker and his nurse there to support him, he made it to the master bathroom and into the tub. He didn't have to lift a finger to wash himself. Asha made sure every inch of him was clean before she helped him to their bed.

It felt good to sleep with him, to know that he had forgiven her and that he loved her still. It felt so good to be close to him again. She would trade whatever riches Lynx had stuffed in the pillowcase for this moment in time.

That night, she slept better than she had since Boom got shot.

CHAPTER 49

THE NEXT MORNING, he was able to sit up against the headrest and enjoy breakfast in bed. Asha served him coffee, waffles, bacon and mixed fruit on a bed tray. While he ate, Boom asked her to sit with him. He had a story to tell.

"This was about five years ago," he began. "I wasn't into confiscating money, but I had a client who didn't want the target killed. He just wanted the man to pay what he owed him. They were both white guys, moving heroin from Mexico. Their business relationship soured, and the man I went after – they called him *Wolf* – didn't wanna break bread and end things on a positive note.

"I had no problem getting a hold of Wolf at his house, but he wasn't scared at all. He knew my client – his name was Harry – he knew Harry would never allow me to kill him. So it wasn't easy to get him to give me the combination to his safe. I tried some of the same shit I usually do, tied him up and started some light torture that got worse over time. When he still wouldn't give up the combination, I decided to waterboard his ass."

Asha frowned.

"Yeah, that's not something I recommend," Boom said, "especially if you don't know what you doing. You can fuck around and kill somebody. The waterboarding went okay, but I didn't know this fool had a fear of drowning. He almost drowned when he was a kid, and that shit had him all shook up. When he decided he didn't want no more, and he would give me the combination, I drug him to the safe and told him to tell me.

"I was standing there waiting for the numbers, so I could open it, but he kept getting it wrong. I thought he was fucking with me, but by then he was scared to death. He swore he couldn't remember the combination."

Asha didn't know where this story was going, but she was intrigued.

"I went back to torturing him," Boom continued. "A nigga like me, I'm thinking he lying, he just don't wanna give up the money. But Wolf swore he was trying to remember. He wanted it to be over. He begged me to take the whole safe. I checked to see if that was an option, but it was bolted to the house from the inside. There was no way I was getting that money without the combination.

"So I called the other guy, Harry, and told him this shit wasn't happening. I told him what Wolf said, about not remembering the combination. I told him a little about what went down, and he told me he believed Wolf. He said I prolly fucked him up so bad, I *traumatized* him, and his brain had the combination locked up somewhere in his head."

At that moment, Asha thought she knew what he was getting at, but she kept listening.

"Harry told me he knew a guy that might be able to help. He said he'd send him to Wolf's house. Now, this other guy is named Nathan Green. He's a real-live *hypnotist*. Like, that's what he do for a living."

Asha's eyes narrowed.

"I know what you thinking," Boom, said, "but that shit worked. I stood right there and watched it. He put Wolf under some kind of trance, and then he started talking about the safe. Wolf looked like he was sleep, but he was responding. And I'll be damned if this nigga didn't give up the combination. I opened the safe and got the money, and that was it. Mission accomplished."

Boom stared at his woman for a few seconds. He had Asha's full attention.

"Here's what I think," he said. "I think you saw who shot me. I think when you say it wasn't Slim or Lynx, you know that for sure, because you saw the shooter. But getting shot at and seeing me get shot traumatized you. So you can't remember what you saw. I still got Nathan's number. I ain't never had to use it, but I keep up with him, just like I keep up with the guy that's got my blood type on deck. You never know when something like that is gon' come in handy.

"Nathan is on the up-and-up now. I can't bring him some beat up, scared motherfucker and make him hypnotize them. But he'll take a client that walks in on their own free will. I wanna call him and tell him to meet with you."

Asha had been waiting patiently to tell him, "Enzo, I don't believe in that."

He nodded. "I know. I didn't either. But I don't see no harm in trying. If it don't work, we ain't lose nothing. But if it do work, you can finally get some closure."

Asha sighed as she watched him. "Enzo, you know what I'ma do if I find out who shot you."

He nodded. "And I ain't gon' be there to help you, or stop you."

"But you still want me to go…"

He continued to nod. His eyes were deathly serious. "I didn't get hit by no stray bullets. Whoever shot me killed Solomon first and then came for me. *On purpose.* If you get a name, and you think you can handle it, then do what you gotta do. I trust your judgement."

She watched him a while longer before rising from the bed and heading to the closet for a disguise.

CHAPTER 50

TWO HOURS LATER, she stopped by Doc's animal hospital and paid him the rest of the money they owed for Boom's care. She added another forty thousand for Tristan. The vet stepped outside and conducted the transaction through the window of the Mustang she chose to drive that day.

"How's he doing?" she asked.

"A lot better than Boom was," Doc informed her. "He's young. Won't take him too long to bounce back. I'll keep him one more night, for observation. Can you bring your van tomorrow?"

She nodded. "Yeah. Same time?"

"That'll work." Before returning to the clinic he said, "I hope this is the end of you and your people getting hurt."

"I'm sure it is. Any more bullets flying won't be coming our way."

"Good. Can't say I won't miss the money, though." He backed away with a Crown Royal bag filled with cash.

"See you tomorrow," Asha told him and put her car in reverse.

CHAPTER 51

THIRTY MINUTES LATER, she entered the office of Nathan Green. A sign on the door labeled him a hypnotist and spiritual healer. His office was a showroom for strange herbs and candles. He even had packs of Tarot cards on the counter next to the cash register, presumably for sale. Asha became more doubtful by the second. The only man in the office was in his mid to late fifties. He wore a short-sleeved button down with Dockers. His hair was short, completely bald on top. His eyes were light blue. He stepped around the counter and greeted her in the foyer.

"Hi, *Kimberly*?" His voice was soft. He reached to shake her hand. His hand was soft as well.

"Hi," Asha said. "Yes, it's me."

Kimberly's hair was styled in a short afro. Her lipstick was bright red. She wore too much mascara. Her blouse was a halter top. She wasn't curvaceous, but her leggings accentuated her slim figure.

Mr. Green released her hand and gestured to a room on her right. "This way."

Inside was a leather recliner with a smaller chair parked next to it. The room was not brightly lit, but it wasn't too dim. The lighting was perfect, as was the decor. It was a lot less distracting than the view she was greeted with when she entered the office.

He told her, "Have a seat."

Asha sat on the recliner but didn't feel comfortable enough to lean back on the leather. Mr. Green sat in the chair next to her.

"I talked to your friend," he said. "Can you tell me more about what brings you here?"

Asha wasn't sure why she suddenly felt apprehensive. "A few days ago, I was in the car with my boyfriend when he got shot," she explained. "I'm starting to feel like I know who did it – like I saw the shooter. But I can't remember. My friend thinks you can help me. But I'll be honest with you, I don't believe in this hypnosis stuff."

He smiled. "It's okay if you're a non-believer, as long as you follow my instructions when I ask you to. Your friend who called me..." His smile faded. "I know him from a long time ago, back when I used to be a different person. He knows I don't do that kind of work anymore."

Asha nodded.

"So, I have to ask you," he said, "what is your plan for the person who shot your boyfriend, if I'm able to help you identify him – or her?"

"I'll give the information to the police," she said with a straight face.

Mr. Green didn't look like he believed her, but he nodded. "Okay, sit back. Try to relax. I'm going to reach over here to recline your chair a little. I want you to be comfortable. I want you to focus on my voice. I can see that you're a little uptight. Are you comfortable?"

After he'd reclined the chair midway, Asha couldn't deny that she was. She nodded and said, "Yes."

"Good. You can keep your eyes open, but I need you to try to clear your mind. Focus on your breathing. Breath in slowly, and hold it for a few seconds before exhaling. I want you to feel how each breath expands your lungs. I want you to become conscious of each breath. Inhale. Hold it. Now exhale, *slowly*... Think about each breath you're taking. Focus on my voice..."

CHAPTER 52

ASHA DIDN'T BELIEVE the man asked her to wake up or anything so dramatic. She didn't think she'd fallen asleep. She certainly didn't feel drowsy. She was aware that a period of time had passed, and Mr. Green had been speaking to her the whole time. She heard the hum of the chair's motor as he returned it to the upright position. Confused, she stared at him oddly. He was staring right back at her.

"What happened?" she asked. "Did it work?"

He nodded, his eyes narrowed.

She couldn't believe it. "I told you who shot my boyfriend?"

He pursed his lips before nodding again. "Yes, you told me."

Asha's heart began to knock. She sat up, leaning forward with her elbows on her knees. She waited for him to divulge the information.

Instead he said, "Kimberly, before we started, I asked what your intentions were for the shooter. I told you I wasn't into the type of activities I once was. I'm responsible for the information I give you. I don't want to be responsible for any harm coming to another individual, even if that person is a murderer. After I got the information you requested, I asked you what you planned to do with the name, if I gave it to you – and you told me the truth."

Asha's eyes widened. She knew the hypnosis must have worked, because she had no recollection of any of that. If he already knew the truth, there was no point in denying it, so she opened her purse, which had been in her lap the whole time.

She asked him, "How much do you charge for a session?"

"It depends. If it's something like tobacco cessation, I charge two hundred per session."

She produced a stack of bills she usually kept for *walking around money*. She knew it was a little less than five thousand. She offered it to him.

With eyes as cold as ice, she told him, "Mr. Green, if you went in my head and found the information I need, then I have a right to know. I understand you wanna keep your hands clean, and I respect that. But you can't pay the bills with your morals. Take this money, and tell me what I told you."

He hesitated for so long, she didn't think he would. But Mr. Green made the decision Boom said he would. He blew out a sigh and took the money.

CHAPTER 53

IT WAS SUNSET when Asha pulled into a lower-class neighborhood on the west side of Overbrook Meadows. She did not have to do any reconnaissance to find her target's home. She'd been there before. The house hadn't changed much in the past couple of years. Asha drove slowly past it and saw that it was still in need of a paint job. The grass out front was overgrown with a few bare spots. There was a late model car in the driveway. The last time Asha saw this car, it had two flats. All of the tires were aired up now, but it still didn't look like the kind of vehicle she'd trust on the freeway.

She didn't know if her target was home and didn't want to kill everyone inside the house, so she continued driving through the neighborhood. The sight of poverty was unnerving, as was her next mission. The people in this community knew *struggle* on a first name basis. Drugs and gangs ran rampant.

She surveyed a few corner stores on one of the busier streets and didn't spot the man she was looking for. At one of the stores, she remembered when Boom had parked across the street and sent her on foot. She remembered questioning a group of men, asking if they knew where to find the man she was looking for today. The memory was bittersweet. At the time, Asha implored her boyfriend not to murder their target. In her opinion, the boy had suffered enough. Since then, he had grown into a man, and the decision to end his life was Asha's alone. Her conscious waged war with her determination as she drove past the stores and turned back into the neighborhood.

At the corner of Ashford and Connecticut, she came upon a park where the community gathered for barbecues on the weekends and basketball on almost every night, usually around this time. Asha pulled to a stop alongside the curb and watched a crowd of eight sweaty men and boys playing a full court game. Her stomach twisted when she spotted KC.

King Cole was eighteen the last time Asha saw him. He had to be twenty or twenty-one now. Topless, and muscular, she'd heard he was the spitting image of his father, King David. She had never seen his father, but she thought Cole shared some physical similarities with his uncle Solomon. She sat expressionless and watched him play basketball, admiring his stamina and agility. She reached into the glove compartment and withdrew a 9mm. It had never been fired, but it was similar to the ones she'd used for her last two jobs. She screwed a silencer onto the weapon, her eyes never leaving the target.

King David, aka KD, was a name Asha had only heard about from Boom. Two years ago, one of KD's rivals hired the bearded monster to end KD's life. Boom completed the hit around the same time he met Asha. It was this job that propelled the murder duo into a bullet riddled mystery and also sparked their romance. Towards the end, they realized someone in KD's family was hunting them. They narrowed the suspects down to his brother Solomon, KD's son Cole or KD's father, Johnny. It turned out Johnny was the culprit. Boom murdered him with his sniper rifle. A mess of pipe bombs under Johnny's wheelchair went off after the fact, leveling his house in spectacular fashion.

Watching Cole now, Asha understood why he'd want to avenge his father and grandfather by going after Boom, but she did not understand why he would kill his own uncle. She observed him run up and down the court until the game ended. It was dark by then, but the lights at the park provided enough illumination to continue playing. With her windows up, she didn't hear Cole decline another game, but she saw him shake his head and walk off the court.

When she and Boom followed him from this very park the last time she was here, Cole walked the short distance towards his home. Tonight, he made his way to a car. It was an older Toyota, in slightly better shape than the junker parked in the driveway of his house. Asha knew this had to be the car she heard speeding away after Solomon and Boom got shot. She was fully confident the hypnotist had pulled the correct name from her subconscious. She could think of no one who had more motive to kill Boom.

Cole got in the car and pulled away from the curb. She gave him a little room before getting behind him.

He drove straight to the house she'd checked when she first arrived in the area. Rather than the driveway, he parked out front. Asha knew he'd bolt when she pulled to a stop directly in front of him, bathing him with her headlights. She knew he'd run because that was what he did when Boom went after him. She hoped he'd run because she did not want to enter his house and have to harm an innocent. She and Boom had already taken too much from this family.

Cole took off, not bothering to close his car door.

Asha slammed the gas pedal and chased him down. She could've run over him in the street, but she waited for him to make his next move. Sure enough, Cole didn't stay on the road for long. He spotted an alleyway and darted into it. Asha pulled over, threw her car in park and hopped out without missing a beat. She ran into the same alley, dodging and hurdling debris as if she'd been there a million times.

Rather than shoot him in the back, she kicked Cole's legs out from under him when she was close enough. He stumbled forward, hitting the ground hard. He rolled quickly to his back and looked up at her. The alley was so dark, she could barely make out the whites of his eyes. But he could see her well enough to know who was after him. Or maybe he recognized her when she was in the Mustang.

Panting, he said, "*I didn't kill you! I could've, but I didn't! I let you live!*"

His voice shaky but strong. Asha was glad it was dark, because her expression belied her resolve. She didn't want this man to die the first time she saw him, and she didn't want him to die now.

"Why'd you do it?" she asked. "Why'd you kill your uncle?"

"*Because he was working with the nigga that killed my dad!*" Cole cried. "*How the fuck could he do that? How could he do that?*"

Asha accepted that. She knew that Cole and Solomon never got along.

"How'd you know?" she asked him. "Who told you?"

"*Everybody knew!*"

"No." She shook her head. "People knew Solomon had a hit list. But they didn't nobody know he hired Boom. You the only one who knew that. Tell me how you knew."

"Why? So you can go kill 'em for trying to help me? They didn't have nothing to do with this! They innocent."

Asha's eyes widened as the last piece of the puzzle came together. Cole didn't have to tell her who told him. She knew.

"I deserved to get revenge for my dad!" he cried. *"Boom killed my dad! And he killed my grandad!"*

The boy sounded so much like his grandfather, it was alarming. She would swear Johnny had said the same thing, right before Boom killed him. She couldn't see Cole's tears, but she could hear them in the quality of his voice.

"I let you live!" he bellowed. *"I could've killed you too, but I didn't! I didn't kill you because you didn't do nothing to me!"* He broke down, crying harder now. *"Why can't you leave me alone...?"*

Tears were sliding down Asha's cheeks as well. Everything Cole said was true. Boom had murdered his father in cold blood. He'd come back and murdered his grandfather. If she murdered Cole, she'd be killing a whole bloodline.

She sniffled. Cole heard it. He sniffled too. Thinking she'd had a change of heart, he began to rise to his feet.

Asha sat him down with five shots from her silenced weapon.

THUMP!THUMP!
THUMP!THUMP!THUMP!

It was too dark to confirm she'd hit him in the head, so she stepped over the writhing body and emptied the rest of her clip, just to be sure.

EPILOGUE

CHAPTER 54

AT TWO A.M. Asha cut the power to her final target's house. A sign posted in the flowerbed out front indicated this home was secured by ADT. Given the neighborhood, Asha had no doubt the sign was not just for show. If her target had notifications from the security system enabled on her phone, she would be informed that the system had been compromised due to a lack of power. But Asha banked on her target being fast asleep. Hopefully the notification wouldn't wake them.

Three minutes after cutting the power, she entered the home. Ten minutes after that, she'd completed her surveillance inside. She hefted a chair in the kitchen and brought it to the target's bedroom. She carefully placed the chair next to the bed, approximately six feet away. She took a seat and watched the woman, who continued to sleep peacefully.

The woman who drove a Lexus with a personalized license plate that read *Ms Thang* didn't awaken until Asha shined a flashlight directly on her face. Initially Ms Thang shielded her eyes and rolled away from the bright light. But then something clicked in her brain, and she realized the light was foreign. She rolled back towards Asha, shielding her eyes from the flashlight, not yet fully awake. Asha turned the light off, and the bedroom, as well as the rest of the house, was completely dark. The woman sat up with a start.

Asha told her, "Don't get out of bed, Michelle."

Prior to entering the home, she didn't know her name. She found the information on a few pieces of mail on the kitchen counter.

Michelle followed her instructions and remained in bed. She looked around anxiously but could see nothing but darkness. Not even the lights from the streetlamps outside penetrated her dark curtains. She reached for her cellphone on the nightstand. It was no longer there. Asha turned the flashlight back on, blinding the woman again.

She said, "Michelle, I need you to calm down."

"*Who are you?*" the woman shrieked. "*What are you doing in my house?*"

Asha moved the light from the woman to herself, so Michelle would know what she was up against. Asha first revealed her left hand, which was resting in her lap. In that hand she clutched a menacing looking pistol.

She asked her, "Do you see what I have in my hand?"

"*Wh, what?*" Michelle was panicked, her eyes wide, but she did not try to get out of the bed.

"Do you see what I have in my hand?" Asha asked again.

"*Yes, what are you – why are you doing this?*"

"The thing screwed on the barrel is a silencer," Asha explained. "I know your neighbors would freak out if they heard a gunshot. In an area like this, the police would come right away. But with this silencer, your neighbors won't hear a thing if I pull the trigger. The good news is I didn't come here to kill you. If I had, you'd be dead by now."

She positioned the light under her chin. Michelle recoiled, understandably freaked out by what she saw. Asha wore a ski mask with night vision goggles that were strapped over and around her head. With the flashlight under her face, she appeared as ghoulish as a Boy Scout telling scary stories near the campfire. The high-tech gear intensified the effect. Asha looked like a well-trained soldier from a special ops unit. She turned off the light, and the room was once again completely dark.

But it wasn't dark for Asha. With the goggles, she could see Michelle clearly. Rather than vibrant colors, her view had a green tint. Even still, she had no problem making out the smallest details in the room, like the terror in Michelle's eyes.

"*Please,*" the woman cried. "*Please don't do this. I don't have anything. Please don't hurt me.*"

"I'm just here to talk," Asha said. "When we get done talking, I'll leave. I promise I won't hurt you, as long as you don't lie to me."

"But I don't know anything. I don't know what you want from me."

"Did you see my goggles?" Asha asked.

"Huh, *what*?"

"Did you see my goggles? I know you can't see me, but you need to know that I can see you very well. Do you understand that I can see you?"

"Wha, what?"

THUMP!

The woman jumped back, as if she'd come upon a snake. She couldn't stop a short scream from escaping her.

"*Wha, what happened*?" She looked around blindly. "*What was that?*"

"I just shot your bed, put a hole in your pillow."

"*Why? Oh my God, what is happening?*"

"I shot at you because you were reaching for your nightstand. If you got a gun in there, believe me when I tell you it won't help you. If you reach for it again, I'ma have to teach you a lesson. You don't want that do you, Michelle? You know if I shoot you in the arm or the hand, you'll start yelling. Your daughter will come in here to see what's wrong, and I'll have to do something to keep her quiet."

"*Don't hurt my daughter!*"

"Lower your voice."

"*Don't you touch her!*"

"I met your daughter two years ago," Asha said, still speaking calmly. "Did Solomon tell you? Me and Boom ran into him at McDonalds. I got in the backseat with your little girl. She's a precious little thing. I didn't hurt her then, and I don't want to hurt her tonight."

Michelle's mouth fell open. Her eyes were nearly as wide. "Oh my God. *It's you.*"

"Yes, it's me. And now that you know who you're dealing with, you should understand that you're alive right now because I want you to be. That could change at any moment."

"*What do you want with me?*" she cried.

"I wanna know why you told Slim about Solomon's hit list. Did you plan for Slim to kill your man, so the two of you could ride off into the sunset?"

"What, I, I don't know what you talking about."

"Michelle, if I have to do something harsh to get you to talk, don't think I won't do it. I know Solomon told you about his hit list, because you're the only one he trusted. He didn't have any partners in his organization. But even careful niggas let their guard down when they with they woman. He was pillow talking his plans to you, and you told Slim. I know you and Slim was fucking. I wanna know if you told him, so he would kill Solomon. Was that your plan?"

Michelle went through a range of emotions right before Asha's eyes. After shock, denial and resentment, she finally acknowledged that the intruder knew way too much. The last emotion she reached was acceptance.

"No," she breathed. "I didn't want Slim to kill Solomon. That's my baby-daddy. Why would I want him killed?"

"What did you think Slim would do when he found out Solomon was trying to kill him, invite him over for a beer?"

"No, but I only told Slim so he could protect hisself. He gave me his word he wouldn't go after Solomon."

The woman was being honest now. Asha kept pushing.

"Did Slim give you his word that he wouldn't tell anyone else about the hitlist?"

She shook her head. "No."

"So it was okay for Pacman or Lynx to go after Solomon, as long as it wasn't Slim. You felt like that was a way to keep yo hands clean?"

Michelle swallowed her guilt and grief before responding. "Slim promised me he wouldn't go after Solomon, and he didn't. He's the only one I had any control over."

Asha accepted that. "What about Cole? What was your reason for telling him about what Solomon had going on?"

The woman hesitated, her mouth open. She closed it and swallowed roughly.

"You doing so good," Asha said. "I appreciate you being honest with me. Don't stop now."

Michelle shook her head slightly. "I, I told him because, I, I thought he had a right to know."

"What did he have a right to know?"

"That, that Solomon was working with Boom. After what Boom did to KD and Johnny. I, I just..." Her breath came in shudders. "I was, I was at they funerals. I was there. I saw how bad Cole was hurt. I couldn't... I told Solomon not to work with Boom. I told him that wasn't right..." Her eyes filled with tears. "He wouldn't listen."

Asha was unmoved. "What did you think Cole would do with the information?"

"He, he said he would try to take Boom out. I – I'm sorry. Please don't kill me. I'm sorry."

"Did you make Cole promise not to hurt Solomon?"

"Wha, *no*. He wouldn't do that. That was his uncle. I knew he wouldn't do anything to Solomon. He, he didn't. *Did he*?"

Rather than tell her the truth, Asha decided to let her stew on that scenario, possibly for the rest of her life. "Well," she said with a sigh, "the only thing left for me to do before I get out of here is get Solomon's money."

"What money? I don't have no money here."

"You know that's not true."

"I don't. I swear to God I don't."

"Michelle, I know Solomon had millions of dollars saved up, and I know it's in this house. You willing to give up your life for that money? If you don't believe nothing else I say, please believe this: I've been through *a lot* because you decided to run yo mouth about Solomon's business. It's a lot of people dead because of you – including yo baby-daddy and yo side nigga. *I am not leaving here without the money*; I promise you that."

"*That's not my money! That's my daughter's money.* That's her inheritance."

"You should've thought about that before you got her daddy killed. If you had kept yo mouth closed, your daughter wouldn't need an inheritance. She'd have her dad and his money. If you think you can get both of the men in your life killed and then slide off like you ain't did nothing wrong, you got another thing coming."

Michelle's face turned to stone. *"I'm not giving you no money,"* she growled. "If you wanna kill me, gone and do it. If I don't do nothing else right, I'ma take care of my daughter. I ain't giving you her inheritance."

"Okay, Michelle. This is where you wanna take a stand, and I respect that. The problem is you don't know who you're dealing with. You said you know who I am, but I can see that you don't.

"Here's what's about to happen: I'm about to shoot you in the kneecaps. *Both of 'em.* You gon' start screaming. I'ma go down the hallway to your daughter's room and snatch her before she tries to run. By then, you'll be trying to crawl down the hallway, but it'll be hard to do that in the dark with no knees. When you make it to your daughter's room, I'll be done hogtying her. I'll leave her on the floor and then tie you up and put tape around your mouth. Then

I'm gon' shine my flashlight on your daughter, so you can watch me cut pieces off her, one at a time.

"The only thing I don't know is how much cutting I'ma have to do, before you change your mind about giving up the money. I'm sure you'll be thinking, *Oh, well, I can get that nose sewed back on,* or *If I style her hair right, people won't notice she don't have an ear.* But eventually, you'll change your mind and give me the money. If not, I'm just gon' say fuck it and kill both of y'all."

She was quiet for a few moments, to let that sink in.

"Before we go that route," Asha continued, "you need to think *real hard* about what you're about to put your baby through. You need to remember that she is the *only* innocent person in this whole equation. She don't deserve to suffer for what you did. I, um, I went to check on her before I came in here. She such a hard sleeper."

Michelle almost jumped out of bed then.

"*Don't you touch her!*"

"Calm down, bitch. I already touched her. But I didn't hurt her." She tossed something onto the bed. She turned her flashlight on, so Michelle could find it.

The woman's hands trembled as she picked up her daughter's pigtail. The braided lock of hair was well over a foot long. Michelle stared at it in horror, cradling it in her hands as if it was her daughter's corpse.

Asha turned the flashlight off, once again shrouding the room in darkness.

"Last chance," she said. "Plan A –show me where the safe is. I done already told you what Plan B is."

"*Uh, oh, okay,*" Michelle said. "Okay. I – I'll show you." She was crying now. "*I'll show you...*"

CHAPTER 55

TWO MONTHS LATER, Asha lie in the center of an enormous bed in a luxurious suite at the Point Pleasant Resort, located in St Thomas, a gateway isle of the Virgin Islands. Her personal masseuse applied suntan lotion to the front side of her body. She basked in his affection, loving the sensation of his strong hands on her breasts, stomach and legs. Caught up in the bliss of the moment, her eyes were mostly closed. She wasn't sure when the application of the lotion turned into a full body massage, but she wasn't mad at all.

Her masseuse was naked, as was she. His dark skin glowed in the dappled sunlight that peaked into their suite from the balcony. The warm, September breeze was like sweet autumn kisses. The sound and scent of the ocean was tantalizing. Asha wished this was where she and Boom planned to live indefinitely, as they sorted out their plans for retirement. But this was merely a vacation – a real one. They had no plans to murder anyone in this region. They had no plans to kill anyone back in the states, either.

As enchanting as their getaway was, moving on from their past sins was easier said than done.

Asha looked up at her man and asked him, "Do you think I'm bad?"

He grinned. The muscles in his chest and arms rippled as he worked his way down her legs, caressing her calves, ankles and even her feet with his magical hands.

He told her, "Roll over." When she complied, he leaned over her and applied lotion to her back. He said, "What do you mean bad? You mean *naked*?"

She smiled slightly. She had her head turned to the side, her eyes closed now. "No. I don't mean naked. I mean *bad*."

"You a bad bitch," he said. "You know that."

"You know that's not what I mean."

"You still tripping about that little girl, ain't you?" he said knowingly.

"Yeah," she acknowledged. "But not just her. I be thinking about what I did to that other lady too. I think her name was Brisha."

"When did you start second guessing yourself?" he wondered.

"You right; it was the little girl that got to me. When you got shot, all I cared about was money. I figured if I got us what we needed to retire, you wouldn't have to be in the streets no more. But it's something about robbing people that don't feel the same. Killing somebody 'cause somebody else want them dead is bad. But killing 'em because I wanna take they stuff – I thought I was okay with it, but now I don't think so. Am I wrong?"

"Nah."

He had worked his way down her body and was rubbing her plump ass now, using the lotion as massage oil. Despite her mixed emotions, she found the sensations erotic.

"I don't know why I'm asking you," she said. "You the last person who can tell me if killing is wrong."

"Hmph. That's cold."

"It's true."

"If it make you feel any better, I think you was right to take Solomon's money."

"Really?"

"For sho'. You ain't have to cut that girl's hair, though."

"*Damn, Enzo.* You see I'm over here struggling with this."

He laughed. "I'm just kidding. It's just hair. It'll grow back."

She frowned and sighed.

"Naw, but on the real," he said, "you put in major work while I was laid up. We had three mil' when I got shot. In three days, you took it upon yourself to get the rest of our retirement money. Now we sitting on more than six mil', and that's after the wash. I appreciate what you did for me – for us. If I can reward you and this pussy every day for the rest of my life, that's what I'm gon' do."

He hiked her ass up and rubbed the head of his dick against her opening before slowly penetrating her. Asha's eyes widened and then closed again as she gripped the sheets and hiked her ass up even more.

"*Yeah, you bad,*" Boom said as he stroked her, deliberately and deeply.

He slapped her ass – *hard*. It sounded off loudly in the quiet room. Asha was shocked by the sudden violence and surprised by how good the stinging pain felt.

"You gon' stop being bad?" he asked, pumping harder now.

Her oasis opened up and began to gush for him.

"*Uhn, uh, yeah,*" she grunted.

"Good girl."

"I mean *no.*"

He slapped her ass again. "Stop being bad."

"*Uh, oh shit.*"

"You gon' stop being bad."

"*Uhn. No.*"

He slapped her other cheek.

"You gon' stop being bad."

"*Uh, uhn, no...*"

He smacked it again. He grinned as he stared down at the cream she was leaving on his dick. He gripped her ass, which had reddened from the slaps, and allowed her control of the rhythm of their lovemaking. She began to grind and throw it back at him.

"Be as bad as you wanna be," he said. "You know that's what I love about you..."

"You don't want me to be good?"

"Only if you want to."

"*I'm, I'm still being bad,*" she breathed.

He reached and grabbed the hair on the back of her head. He pulled back, and her head was forced to follow.

She cried out in pleasure, or maybe it was pain.

"*Aaah!*"

His dick was rock hard, but it grew even harder. He couldn't wait to see what it would take for her to decide that maybe she wanted to be good after all.

KEITH THOMAS WALKER

ABOUT THE AUTHOR

Keith Thomas Walker, known as the Master of Romantic Suspense and Urban Fiction, is the author of more than two dozen novels, including *Fixin' Tyrone*, *Life After*, *The Realest Ever*, the *Backslide* series, the *Brick House* series, the *Finley High* series and the *Asha and Boom* series. Keith's books transcend all genres. He has published romance, urban fiction, mystery/thriller, teen/young adult, Christian, poetry and erotica. Originally from Fort Worth, he is a graduate of Texas Wesleyan University. Keith has won numerous awards in the categories of "Best Male Author," "Best Romance," "Best Urban Fiction," "Best Young Adult Romance," "Best Duo," "Book of the Year," and "Author of the Year," from several book clubs and organizations. Visit him at www.keiththomaswalker.com.